I0762860

Praise for *Small Boat*

"A gut-punch of a novel. . . . *Small Boat* explores the power of the individual and asks us to consider the havoc we may cause others, the extent to which our complacency makes us complicit—and whether we could all do better."

—2025 Booker Prize judges

"We are all reflected in the complex, unlikable, utterly human, and nearly redeemable protagonist of the brilliant, slim novel *Small Boat*. This story of migrants drowning in the English Channel is a must-read book of our time—this time in which we daily bear witness to a multitude of preventable tragedies just across our phone screens and, like Delecroix's rescue-operative narrator, convince ourselves that we are helpless to act."

—Hannah Lillith Assadi, author of *Sonora*
and *The Stars Are Not Yet Bells*

"Shocking and unsettling, *Small Boat* is an unforgettable modern tragedy."

—Paula Hawkins

"This book challenged me profoundly. It moved me, and stayed with me. It's not an easy read—but as our politics descend into hate-mongering and point-scoring, it's an essential story that needs to be told."

—Dua Lipa

"Vividly translated, *Small Boat* is painful, compelling, and mercifully short, with a powerful undertow."

—*The Times Literary Supplement*

"Delecroix is both a novelist and a Kierkegaard expert: both pursuits lend themselves to the imagination of ethics at crisis point. Think of *Small Boat* as a philosophical ghost story."

—*The Telegraph*

"The narrator accuses those who judge her of hypocrisy and will only see herself as a cog in the administrative wheel of a France that will not give refuge to the world's misery. As strong and cruel as the times we live in."

—*Paris Match*

"A work of sickening power, it's won a deserved place on the International Booker short list."

—*Daily Mail*

"A powerful reimagining of a migrant tragedy."

—*Financial Times*

"A work of striking empathy."

—*Monocle*

SMALL BOAT

SMALL BOAT

VINCENT DELECROIX

Translated by Helen Stevenson

MARINER BOOKS

New York Boston

This novel is inspired by a true story that was widely reported in the press. With the exception of the elements of this news item known to the public, the following text is a work of pure fiction.

HarperCollins books may be purchased for educational, business, or sales promotional use. For information, please email the Special Markets Department at SPsales@harpercollins.com.

The Mariner flag design is a registered trademark of HarperCollins Publishers LLC.

hc.com

Originally published as *Naufrage* in France in 2023 by Éditions Gallimard.

This translated edition was first published in 2025 by Small Axes, an imprint of HopeRoad.

FIRST US EDITION

Library of Congress Cataloging-in-Publication Data has been applied for.

ISBN 978-0-06-349169-4

Printed in the United States of America

26 27 28 29 30 LBC 5 4 3 2 1

CONTENTS

AUTHOR'S NOTE

This novel is inspired by a true story that was widely reported in the press. With the exception of the elements of this news item known to the public, the following text is a work of pure fiction.

INTRODUCTION

In November 2021 more small boats attempted the Channel crossing from France to the UK than in any other month before or since, with around seven thousand asylum seekers on board. Not all made it across; some met with disaster. According to HM Coastguard, more than 750 people put out from France on the night of 23/24 November. The UK's Border Force rescued nearly a hundred in British waters after three of the boats foundered. Another, containing at least thirty migrants, capsized on the same night, in an inflatable dinghy with an outboard motor, launched on the 23rd at roughly 9 p.m. from a beach near Dunkirk. Within a few hours at sea, it was taking in water and the inflatable collar was leaking air.

Once a small boat in the Channel is in trouble, migrants use mobile phones to raise the alarm, preferably with rescue services in the UK, their destination. Under no circumstances, barring catastrophe, do they want to be returned to France if they can help it. Nor do the French authorities want to tow them back and have them lingering on the coast for another opportunity to cross. But in extreme danger they will call the French 'regional monitoring and rescue centre', known as the CROSS, at Cap Gris-Nez, half an hour's drive down the coast from Calais.

On 24 November, between midnight and 1 a.m.,

staff at the CROSS in Cap Gris-Nez logged a call from their British counterparts saying that a small boat was in trouble in French waters. At roughly 1.45 a.m. the CROSS received a desperate message from the passengers on the boat, who explained that it was 'broken'. They sent their geolocation via WhatsApp, which put them in French waters, and the team at Cap Gris-Nez decided against a rescue mission. Instead, they called the Coastguard at Dover: the boat in question, they reported, was about 0.6 nautical miles (just over a kilometre) from British waters. Then, after updating the boat's geolocation, they contacted Dover again at about 2.30 a.m. to say that it was now 'in your zone'. But calls kept arriving at the CROSS from the terrified passengers. One of them explained that he was now 'in the water'. The CROSS radio operator replied: 'Yes, but you're in English waters.'

This was one of more than a dozen exchanges in a two-hour period ending at roughly 4.25 a.m. In that time a French trawler, whose crew spotted the migrant boat, alerted the CROSS and asked for guidance. They were told that a French rescue vessel, *Flamant*, was already heading towards it. At roughly the same time, *Flamant* notified the CROSS that a UK Border Force cutter was making for the scene. The Coastguard in Dover informed the CROSS that it was 35 to 40 minutes away and that *Flamant* was much closer. In the event, *Flamant* hung back.

There were many small boats in the Channel that night. As the minutes ticked away, several mobile calls from different numbers had misled the Dover Coastguard into thinking they were in contact with more than one boat in distress, before they realised that the calls were coming from the same doomed dinghy.

Even so, it was hard to know for sure that the Border Force cutter was heading for the right boat. In due course, when they arrived at its likeliest position, there was no sign of it.

There were other small boats crammed with migrants in the search zone and the crew of the cutter soon found they had their hands full. Monitoring the search in British waters from Cap Gris-Nez, French duty officers may have breathed a sigh of relief. Surely the UK Border Force were now assisting the people who had been pleading for their lives for the better part of three hours. Just after 5 a.m. the CROSS signed off on the dinghy with an entry in the incident log. 'Rescued.'

On the afternoon of the 24th the crew of a fishing boat spotted bodies floating in French waters. A search began and eventually 27 were recovered. Most of the dead were Iraqi Kurds, including four women; among the rest were Afghans and Ethiopians, a Somali woman and three other men, one identified as Vietnamese, another as Egyptian, a third as an Iranian of Kurdish origin. The body of another passenger, an Iraqi Kurd, was not found. There may have been others. It was the largest single loss of life in the Channel since the pioneers of a new migrant pathway to the UK set off in boats from the French coast in 2018.

There were strong reactions on both sides of the Channel. First the handwringing, followed swiftly by a search for someone to call to account. People smugglers were the obvious culprits. In France, the UK also came under criticism for luring migrants into the grey economies of the Anglosphere to work for a pittance. In the shadow of these vague charges, the British Marine Accident and Investigation Branch produced a detailed report, which pointed to shortcomings on the part of the Coastguard.

In France, a lengthy inquiry was opened by a branch of the police. Staff on duty at the CROSS on the night of 23/24 November were summoned for interview.

The police had recordings of the exchanges between Cap Gris-Nez and the migrant boat, as well as off-microphone comments made by the operator as she cut away from the migrants and spoke in private to herself or her colleagues in the control room. 'Don't you get it? You won't be saved. "I'm up to my feet in water"? It wasn't me who told you to leave.' There was worse. According to the British report, the CROSS had told the Dover Coastguard that *Flamant* was unavailable at the decisive moment because it was assisting other small boats in French waters. No reliable media source in France could confirm this.

The events of the night come to us as a forensic narrative that relies on precise times, recorded exchanges and geolocation imagery saved to hard drives. Like the investigators, we can imagine that some of the findings are slippery without casting doubt on the whole edifice. The press and the authorities in France continued to probe long after the incident, and in 2023 an investigating judge opened a file on five staffers at Cap Gris-Nez and two of the crew of *Flamant*, on suspicion of 'failure to assist persons in danger'.

The Channel crossing is much more dangerous than it looks. Overall numbers of dead and missing migrants who have tried to reach the UK from France by lorry, on foot through the Channel tunnel or by sea since 2014 are put by the International Organisation for Migration at around three hundred. Of those at least 80 drowned, but the figure is surely higher. In 2024, 78 people lost their lives attempting the journey in small boats. More than 90 per cent of those who have reached the UK from

France since 2018 claimed asylum; roughly 75 per cent were successful. All the more reason to consider the fate of those who died in the attempt and determine the proximate cause of their deaths.

—

Vincent Delecroix's compelling novel raises the unsettling possibility that each of us is complicit in the suffering of migrants. A philosopher specialising in Kierkegaard, Delecroix has written several non-academic essays and works of fiction. But as he warns in his novel *Ascension* (2017), 'a vague propensity to make things up isn't enough to earn the right – and I mean the right – to legitimacy, permission to write literature and novels in particular.' In this excellent translation by Helen Stevenson, a long debate about guilt and innocence unfolds in the mind of the narrator, a radio operator at Cap Gris-Nez, as she is questioned by a policewoman about the fateful night. Some elements are drawn from the public record, many more from the author's imagination. In the opening scene, the narrator confronts her interrogator, a steely, mirror likeness of herself, with the same 'coat hanger' shoulders. Hearing her own voice played back from seized recordings unsettles her. It's clear to her, and to French public opinion, that she has failed in her duty as a rescue worker, yet she suspects she is also being taken to task for a moral shortcoming. Perhaps she is indifferent to the lives of people on small boats.

But she is a rescue operative, she protests to her likeness, trained 'precisely not to have convictions or a conscience': she is not supposed to discriminate between a trawler in distress, a billionaire's yacht or a foundering migrant boat. Her interrogator presses her. 'Can you not see the difference between an irresponsible pleasure tripper and a dinghy full of migrants?' 'Should I be more intent on saving some than others?' Not necessarily, says her mirror-image, but how could she fail to distinguish 'the causes of their being in this situation'? Is she now being accused of prioritising 'a rich guy showing off' to his guests over 'a handful of Iraqi Kurds'? 'I failed to make a distinction when I should have,' she concludes, 'and when I shouldn't have made a distinction I did.'

While she's fielding these questions, we learn that she is the single mother of a young girl; that she is separated from the father, who has no patience with rescuing migrants at sea ('how much does this bullshit cost us?'); that she runs on the beach to decompress; and that one of her colleagues on the night-watch feigns serene indifference when he fields distress calls. She can't share his affectation of 'noble despair'. Having loved the sea when she was young, she is now in awe of it: it is 'always with me', a force of unambiguous harm, 'glutted with women and children'. She feels its hunger whether she's staring at a bank of monitors or running on the sand, and suspects that it wants to swallow the ground beneath her, surging inland, engulfing the continent, everything.

Living on a fragile shoreline, she is also conscious of the porous margin between accountability and blame. She has been suspended from her job and is now under suspicion of negligence in the matter of 27 migrants lost at sea. But should she assume the immense burden of blame for these deaths? A recording of her words comes back to haunt her: 'You will not be saved.' Whether or not the migrants heard them is far less important in this novel than the fact that they were uttered in the first place and are now in the public domain.

This, we're left to imagine, may have been the

narrator's darkest transgression: to have denied the comforting assurance of rescue, not just to the passengers on the boat but to untold numbers of observers, who prefer to think that all will be well, 'so that humanity... need not doubt its humanity' – and that they, too, will be rescued. Even her interrogator is shocked by the recording. Had she promised to 'save' the passengers on the boat, the narrator thinks, things would have turned out differently: a few words spoken in bad faith would have let her off the hook.

Standing at the sea's edge, she looks behind her at a vast hinterland in which one obstacle after another conspires against the lives of people who have covered great distances to take the final gamble. And again she thinks of those who look on, not in the way she was trained to look, but as rapt observers of disaster, anguished yet mysteriously absolved. As she turns once more to the sea, she imagines 'all the others at my back... millions of people. The entire world is there... There is no shipwreck without spectators.' Are they really blameless?

Jeremy Harding

Suave mari magno turbantibus aequora ventis,
E terra magnum alterius spectare laborem*

— Lucretius

'You are embarked'

— Pascal

*Pleasant it is, when on the great sea the winds trouble the waters,
to gaze from the shore upon another's great tribulation

I didn't ask you to leave, I said.

It was your idea, and if you didn't want to get your feet wet, love, you shouldn't have embarked. I didn't push you into the water, I didn't fetch you from your village or field or ruin of a suburb and put you in your wretched leaky boat, and now the water's up to your ankles, I get it that you're frightened, and you want me to save you and you're impatient. You're counting on me. But I didn't ask you for any of that. So you'll just have to grin and bear it and let me get on with my job.

And apparently these thoughts were so strong that I actually spoke them out loud, the first bit, at least, certainly if the recordings are to be believed and there's no reason not to believe them. I accept that.

While I was at it I should perhaps have added things like 'I'm not God Almighty either', which must have been what was in my mind, and I could have actually said it. I could have said 'There are guys like you everywhere tonight, forty small boats supposedly sinking at the same time in the Channel and I can't see to everyone at once. So you'll have to be patient, love, or tell all the others that are sinking to calm down and get off their phones so I can just look after you; you go ahead and call all the others, since you've got a phone, all those people climbing into battered old boats with no compass or flares, thirty at once on a raft that can scarcely take the weight of five, no instruments, nothing to steer by, no knowledge of the sea, along with their women and children.

But in the end I said to Julien, who was next to me: These guys are unbelievable, one minute they jump in the water, the next they're practically shouting at you for not throwing them the lifebuoy fast enough, cheeky, I call it. He smiled and plunged back into his book. Leaky, more like, he remarked. That's the sort of joke that raised a laugh at 3 a.m.

That joke didn't get recorded; it probably wouldn't have looked too good, and Julien can rest easy: no one's going to call him a monster for making a joke about inflatable dinghies springing leaks. Besides, on the phone recordings you can only hear my voice, unluckily for me.

After that I went back to my screens, my PC, my microphone, thinking surely they should be happy; they wanted to get to England, they're there now, in British waters, in a British vessel by now, wrapped up like sweeties in gold paper; they can continue their conversation in English to their hearts' content.

But in the end the currents brought their bodies back into French waters.

So now they were floating on the investigator's desk, at the Coast Guard office. There were twenty-seven of them to be exact, including a little girl, scattered among the ballpoint pens, the note blocks, folders, floating round the police inspector's computer, including also the body of the man who had called me fourteen times that night and who now, obviously, had fallen silent. The sea was calm on the surface of the desk, no wind, no swell, and alongside the bodies only orderly piles of paper.

While she was playing me the recordings, the policewoman sometimes stared hard at me, sometimes gazed out of the window at I know not what, because from my signal station all I ever saw was the sea, and given a choice I would much rather, like today, look out at a stretch of road with a building site, some workers, Africans mostly, but at least they were alive, not wet and chilled to the bone, not women, not children, so I was ok looking at all that, while they played me the recording of the voice saying Please, please and me saying Calm down, help is coming.

The policewoman wore her hair tied back severely in a pony tail, exactly like me, I thought, and sat up straight like me, a bit like a soldier, with coat-rack shoulders as Eric used to say, the same look, if that makes sense, but ten years older, her in her blue police pullover and me in my own clothes, obviously, a ridiculous sweatshirt, and trainers, as though I'd just come back from my morning run, looking like a kid even with my severe pony tail, like some sulky, stony-faced school kid summoned before the head teacher. And I expect it was this absurd and vaguely humiliating resemblance, this caricature, this depressing, unsparing image of what I must actually look like, staring me in the face, that made it so hard for me to like her, so easy to dislike, in fact, though in any case there was no question, in this situation, of liking her.

As she showed me into her office she had said, Thank you for coming of your own accord, your boss has so far refused to give us your contact details. She added, Your colleague, apparently, the one on duty with you that night, has not shown a similar – the same – but she hesitated over what should come next, Conscientiousness perhaps, or maybe Courage, or even Moral Scruple, or Sense of Duty, but she couldn't find quite the right words, so she corrected herself saying, 'Has not chosen to do so, as yet.'

And, fortunately, she did not ask me why I *had* chosen to take this step, as she finally put it, and why I had turned up like this of my own free will, before the judge and quite possibly the police came to my house anyway to take me away in front of my little girl and put me in the dock on a charge of failure to assist a person in danger or some such; anyway, fortunately, she did not ask me why, after dropping Léa off with my parents that morning, I had got in my car and driven to the coastguard station at Cherbourg, a four-hour drive from Boulogne, a motorway stop for an insipid coffee, on the surface of which I saw little dinghies bobbing about but actually they were biscuit crumbs, and all around me people silently pointing at me behind my back, a call to my parents to check everything was ok with my daughter, if she was upset about not going to school, another to the police to say I'm coming, I'm on the road, surprised when they don't answer in English at the other end, no voice saying Please, please, no one screaming in the background, just We will wait for *you*, as reasonable shipwrecked people should have said, sitting it out quietly, since there wasn't much else they could do anyway except pray and keep their eyes peeled for a boat. We will wait for you, they would have said calmly, instead of continuing their endless, pointless pleading, refusing to understand the difference between being in French waters and being in British waters – instead of calling fourteen times in two hours to say they were sinking, instead of annoying me by saying it over and over again, as if it was me that didn't understand, when I did. I understood perfectly, your feet are in the water but it's English water, not French, and yes I know they're both equally cold, so set your sights in that direction if you still know your north from your south.

Lucky then that she didn't ask me why I'd finally decided to come, because I wouldn't have known what to say, though I'm pretty sure I wouldn't have used words like Moral Scruple or Sense of Duty, definitely not Courage, words like Exhaustion and Nausea more likely, and definitely Anger like Shame.

It was also that I wanted to hear myself. I mean hear and not read myself, read my words in the newspaper, hear my own voice and not the voice of the journalists repeating on the television what I said, alongside expressions like migrant drama, migrant tragedy, as though every evening at eight o' clock we were at the theatre and they were putting on the same play, and it really is the same play, with me in the front row – I never miss a performance, I show up every evening for the migrant drama; they give me a free seat and even pay me for it; some people are in boxes, some in the gallery, but they give me a look-out post in the front row so I can see clearly; that way, I'm both in the front row *and* in the dress circle looking out at the sea, and even if the title of the play varies – sometimes Migrant Drama, sometimes Migrant Tragedy, Drama in the Channel, or sometimes Drama in the Mediterranean – of course it's always the same play, and always the same character, and at one point the character picks up a phone to address the audience. It's interactive, he calls out to them, it starts with Please, please, but he's not really addressing the audience, who meanwhile are gasping oh and ah and sometimes sighing with indignation, it's me, just me, he's talking to. It's for me to answer, and answer well, or the audience isn't happy, and the sighs of indignation are for me, and the next day the theatre critics lay into me, because my responses determine how the play unfolds, and if I do a good job the Migrant Drama is a bit less of a Migrant Drama, not to mention the fact that at the same time I have to sort out what's happening on other stages where they're showing the Drifting Yacht Drama, or the Capsized Trawler Tragedy.

To hear myself, then, hear my own voice, right here in the Coast Guard's office, to be absolutely sure of what I said instead of hearing some dolled-up journalist parroting that I'd said this, that and the next thing – including *horrible* things, *scandalous* things, or *shocking* things, and going on to say that I had done or had not done things that I should or shouldn't have.

But it was mostly him you heard on the recordings. I don't know what to call him – the Migrant, Telephone Man, Sinking Man, but I knew his voice by heart, what he was saying, too, because in reality it's always the same man calling. Every night, the same voice, the same pleas, because it doesn't matter how many times you pull this idiot out of the water, back he comes – one time, ten times, a hundred times. One night you pull him out when he's drowning and he's safe and sound, he might even thank you, and the next night he's calling back again, because he's in the water again, as though he didn't learn his lesson and he's saying, Please, please. Every day you set him back on dry land and every night he's back again and it feels like it will go on this way till Judgement Day – the same guy, every time, back in the water, drowning in mid-Channel, waiting to be rescued, so he can do it again the next night, and eventually it's wearing.

But my voice too, though it wasn't quite my voice, not because the recording inevitably distorts the tone, but because it was my professional voice, the one that crisply handles the nightly disaster with phrases like Calm down and Send me your geolocation by WhatsApp or Help is coming. So we heard mostly phrases of this kind at 2.05, 2.36, 3.12, 4.22 right up till 4.32, after which we heard nothing more, and among these phrases there were others which I apparently should not have uttered, like when I said I didn't ask you to leave and the investigator asked me what to make of that particular phrase.

So I told the investigator that in my opinion they shouldn't attach too much importance to that particular phrase – since it was clearly a problem – even though I didn't know if they were going to send me to prison for stating the blindingly obvious – namely that it really wasn't me that asked them to leave, if that was one of the mistakes they were accusing me of, but what mistake exactly? Because after all, I might have said that to any irresponsible person out sailing, to the cretin who takes to the waves regardless of the weather conditions or doesn't know how to handle their dumb little sailboat and is gobsmacked to find themselves in trouble, and panics and the entire French Navy has to be called out so they don't get a dunking. And if *he* tried telling me I'm not acting fast enough, as though what's happening to him is my fault, I'd tell him the same thing, that it wasn't me that asked him to leave, after all.

But she looked at me, as though she didn't believe me and I had a moment of doubt myself. But why?

Sensing this, she asked sneakily Can you not see the difference between an irresponsible pleasure tripper and a dinghy full of migrants? It was not the most well-meaning question, but actually it was quite easy to answer because my profession requires us to make no distinction, so that's what I said, and that I should be congratulated for not making one: you rescue everyone without distinction. Should I be more intent on saving some more than others?

But that wasn't what she meant, of course, because I seemed to somehow think that some hick who sets out to sea with a leak in his pleasure boat and people fleeing poverty and war were the same thing, as though they were all in the same boat, on a fishing trip. The distinction to be made was not between one man who's drowning and another man who's drowning, but between the reasons, how they came to be in this situation. The distinction to be made is why people leave, why thirty people might set out in a little nut shell and not all alone in their First 24. So the problem actually was that I *didn't* make a distinction, that I didn't appear to grasp that every situation is different, that not everyone sets out in the same way, and certainly not for the same reasons, and therefore not under the same conditions.

However, this insidious question implied that, on the

contrary, I actually was making a distinction, but in the wrong direction. In other words I would ultimately have been keener to save some rich guy showing off on his yacht on a stormy night than on calling out help for a handful of Iraqi Kurds who insist on splashing about in the Channel every night. In other words, I failed to make a distinction when I should have, and when I shouldn't have made a distinction, I did, and there was only one possible reason for that, and it was the same one. And since she was clearly about to end up asking me if I had a grudge against the migrants, or if I considered the life of a migrant of lesser value than that of a yachtsman or a company boss on a fishing spree, in order to head off a question of that kind, I said that I held no opinion on the migrants. I had no more opinion on the migrants than I did on migration policy or the right to asylum, relations between North and South, problems, solutions, the woes of the world, injustice: I was not required to have an opinion on the migrants.

Honestly, I have no opinions about the migrants; in fact, I have even less of an opinion about them than other people, I imagine, and in fact I am *required* to have none, and that's fine by me. If anyone has opinions about the migrants it's my ex, Léa's dad; he's got plenty, and they're pretty much the same as those of the baker on the corner and the checkout women at the local supermarket, who I sometimes chat with on my a week off. Pretty much the same, in fact, as those of half of Calais, Boulogne and Dunkerque. Working at the CROSS meant I got to hear even more of Eric's views on the migrants, because not only could he not see why we went to so much trouble, at the CROSS, to come to the aid of these parasites, and why, as soon as we spotted one, we didn't chuck them straight in the water, with a good thwack of an oar if possible, to make sure they didn't rise back up to the surface.

It had all started with stories about Calais and the Jungle, because Calais was where Eric came from, and by the end he just couldn't bear the thought of me doing that job, rescuing trawlers and cargo ships, yes, rescuing migrants, no. Every time I got home he'd ask how many did you fish out of the water this time, and how much does this bullshit cost us, and why don't you push them over into English waters and let them get on with it if they're determined to get there, and why, once you've fished them out, don't you send them straight to Africa. Don't you think we've got better things to do than kiss them better? They should look after themselves or stay at home. I'd heard it a thousand times, until, for reasons that actually had nothing to with that, I asked him to leave, once and for all. I was not there to tell the story of my life with Léa's dad and how we ended up separating.

(Is that why I came here, I wondered: to talk about the Migrant Drama? Is that the object of this enquiry: what I think about the migrants? As though I wasn't in an office at a police station, but in a television studio, to express my views and be judged on them, i.e. was I bothered about the famous Migrant Drama, showing nightly in the Channel, the Mediterranean, Ceuta or Lesbos? What did I think about the Calais jungle, did I think installing showers and toilet blocks in the camps rendered them dangerously attractive?)

For sure, I might well hold opinions on these subjects. I might well have a view, or have formed one, as they say, given that every day I have the dregs of the earth spilling out before my eyes, stagnating for a while in Calais, in Grande-Synthe, then throwing themselves into the sea – all these people who think we owe them something because they're dying of hunger in their own countries, or simply because they want their own car and might be entitled to it, who come looking for the blanket of universal health care and are lucky if they find a survival blanket. But I don't have opinions of that kind because it wouldn't be professional and, unlike Julien, who is almost always my partner in the rescue group, I don't even assume that absence of opinion – which is an opinion in itself – when he looks down from *on high* or *askance* at all the trivial, tragic turbulence out there in the Channel, affecting the indifference of a world-weary sage, an air of couldn't-care-less as he reads his book when the weather is calm. And I'd even have to say I had no *views* on the matter; I'll leave that to other people, who have plenty. That way they won't have to worry about life belts. It's not that I don't know what to think about the Migrant Drama, the Migrant Tragedy, the Shipwreck of Europe, the Graveyard of the Mediterranean or the Channel – to employ all those received journalistic expressions that simply disgust me – it's not that I don't know what to think, it's that I don't have any thoughts about them at all.

I'm not running an NGO. I'm not there to defend a cause and I don't send help because it's *right*; that's what I needed to say to the police inspector, to get her to understand. It's not my moral conscience or whatever, that throws life belts or survival blankets.

So I have no opinions, I said again, at least, not opinions

on *that* matter, no particular convictions, nor should I, because I'm paid to monitor maritime traffic and co-ordinate rescue if necessary, not to have convictions, one way or another. I can't think why I would need to have convictions, one way or another, to do this job; if I did, it really would be a disaster. Likewise, if I let my conscience trouble me, because having a conscience stops you acting, making decisions, being effective. That's a given, and it's the first thing they teach you in this job. I'm required precisely *not* to have convictions or a conscience. And you are the last person, I concluded, of all people, who can contradict me on that, because I'm sure that if one of your police colleagues had a conscience you'd consider it a professional weakness.

So I didn't enlist with the Navy to save the migrants sloshing about on the rail tracks of Pas-de-Calais, that's for sure, but if I'm asked to do it, or to help do it, I do. So don't then ask me what I think, deep down, about these people, or rather about their obsession with flinging themselves into the water in search of I know not what. Also, I have to do it with the means available, and that's something we might talk about, the means available, or rather the lack of means available for carrying out these missions, because this lack of means available might actually have something to do with what happened, seeing as how I cannot send out dozens of dinghies, speedboats, patrol boats or forty helicopters to save forty small boats at the same time. You have to prioritise.

Yes, but the fact is you didn't send anyone at all, she interrupted, and in the end that, she added, was what I needed to explain. That was why we were there: to explain why they had spent three hours sinking when there was a patrol boat twenty kilometres away, why even once the English had been alerted, no one (i.e. not me) had informed them that the small boat was in trouble; why when a ship spotted them and asked me what to do, I had told them they should just carry on, take no notice. Why I had lied to the migrants for almost three hours. And with a gesture of annoyance she played the recordings again, and ten times over I heard myself say Calm down help is coming, admittedly in an increasingly irritable tone, because they just didn't understand, they were so caught up in their terror, their obtuse despair, caught up in not wanting to die, with staving off the night that was consuming them, the water that was grabbing their ankles and dragging them down into the deep. And they started to sink all over again in the piercing cold night as I looked out of the window at the workers busy on the building site opposite.

But the more I said Calm down and then First, I need your position, and Yes, but now you are in English waters you must call 999, the more it seemed to me that the sea, incomprehensibly, had begun to encroach on the building site opposite the police station window, so that soon the living Africans would also have their feet in the water and be calling for help.

I decided instead to listen to my daughter's voice, and that's what I did, forgetting the recordings, because at least she doesn't ask me in English to save her every night, and I don't need to – she's not in danger of drowning in her little bed at night or in her bowl of hot chocolate in the morning. The night isn't threatening to swallow her, and when she holds out her arms to me, it's not so I'll get her out of there, and when I tuck her in, it's not with a survival blanket, and when I lie down next to her in the evening, when I hold her tight to warm her up and send her to sleep, burying my face in her neck, I don't feel her shivering with cold and terror.

But my daughter said nothing. She was sleeping, and in her bedroom you could hear a voice from the depths of the night saying Please save us, so then I had to hold my daughter even tighter, so that the imploring cries didn't wake her, to murmur in her ear not to worry, go back to sleep, everything was fine. She stirred in her sleep, pressed up against me, but now there were more cries. I was waiting for them to stop, once and for all, but back they came, so I had to cover her ears, cover them so everyone would go back to sleep, which I was about to do myself when the voice of the police inspector spoke in my daughter's bedroom, too, saying, Madame, are you still with us or are you day-dreaming? Because I clearly hadn't paid as much attention as I should have to the recordings, and instead had gone into a daydream, watching the workers on the construction site, who were now doing their best to struggle against the rising water.

(I hadn't even noticed that during this time another policeman had come into the room, and was standing there with his back to the wall opposite the window with his arms folded, listening to the recording with his colleague, watching me in silence.)

The police inspector wanted to establish the sequence of events once and for all, as she put it, on which basis we could finally get down to discussing the essential.

We're not listening to this just to make you feel bad, she tried to assure me, in a gentler tone, she was simply trying, she insisted, to shed some light on what had happened. I had to smile because *shed some light on* seemed to me a particularly unfortunate expression, seeing as how it is precisely at night, in the deep dark of night, that everything happens. Shed some light, I murmured, is exactly what we need to do.

But, on the contrary, it was dark and it was night, since it was one in the morning, and at one in the morning the English contacted us about a small boat that was adrift, and forty-eight minutes later the occupants of the boat themselves called us asking for help. According to the GPS, it's true, they were in French waters, but the currents were pushing them into English waters, so I called the English back to warn them they were approaching, and I told the occupants of the small boat not to panic because the rescue services were on their way. There was no sound of an engine – theirs must have broken down – and the dinghy might be drifting and perhaps it was filling with water, and when an hour later they did actually find themselves in English waters, I called the English again to inform them, and the English, as far as I know, mobilised a patrol boat but since they were forty-five minutes away they asked us to send a patrol boat to the area, too. This was not possible since our boat was busy on another mission, and from then on the occupants of the dinghy kept on and on calling, saying the dinghy was broken, it was filling with water, we must help them, we must come and save them, etc…but no one did save them and the English did not find them. They sank, apparently and drowned, twenty-seven of the twenty-nine of them. Two survived. End of story.

—

End of story, indeed, sighed the police inspector, not looking particularly satisfied with my version of events. Which was confirmed when she observed that I had presented all that, in her opinion, without much sympathy, and, if the truth be told, with an astounding degree of detachment. But I couldn't see what it would have added if I had spoken elegantly, or brought my personal feelings, which in any case I didn't have, into what was, after all, supposed to be simply an objective account of the facts. What difference would it have made if I'd said *those poor people* instead of *them*, for example? Besides, I added, the whole exercise seemed superfluous to me, seeing as she knew very well what had happened, the sequence of events, as she put it. But, apparently, she wanted to hear my version of events or rather, she corrected, she wanted to hear how I'd experienced them.

So I replied that the whole point was that I'd laid out the facts in the way I'd experienced them, at which she looked even more concerned and glanced at her colleague, who still had not spoken. She asked if I wanted a coffee.

Without waiting for my response, she left the office together with the other police officer, leaving me looking out at the construction site opposite – which this time was deserted, no water either (I must have been imagining things); it must be their lunch break. And my eyes started wandering round the room, the shelves and cupboards, the incomprehensible posters, the files, things you could equally well have found in the operations room at the CROSS, and the surface of the desk from which the drowned people had vanished, thank God, while I was beginning to think that I had better go home and pick Léa up from my parents because, to be honest, we'd pretty much covered everything here. I'm coming home, I said to Léa, I'll just say goodbye to the police inspector. We're done; I'm on my way back now, we'll have tea at home. Don't worry about your homework being late.

Right, said the police inspector when she came back into the room without her acolyte, placing her coffee on the table, there's no point digging your heels in; you're not on trial here, you understand that? And she added that the sole point of the investigation was to establish if there had been negligence, and that was why she wanted to go over everything with me. She'd now adopted a teacherly sort of tone, as though she was addressing a retarded child, but what was evident, anyway, was that in her administrative parlance *negligence* basically meant *my* negligence, and I recalled that a few days after the opening of the legal investigation, Julien had also used the word *negligence*

Over a beer by the port, Julien said to me, Don't stress, nothing's going to happen to you. No one gets sent to prison because they made a misjudgement and there was some negligence. But negligence in what, and who was this they, I asked him, who misjudged the situation: the fifty people we work with every day? The six duty teams? You and me? To which he didn't respond, probably because *you and me* was already quite a lot – to be precise it was one too many to amount to a *they* that matched the situation, and might walk into a police station or the judge's office, a *they* who had been negligent and who therefore could be regarded as the actual Wrecker.

I didn't much like the idea of being trapped all alone in this *they*, while Julien carried on drinking beers and watching trawlers come back into port, with his perpetual half-smile, and his blasted book beside his glass of beer – the one he was peacefully immersed in that night while I responded to voices that already were posthumous. It's the book he always carries round with him when he's on night duty, playing the detached intellectual. But when all was said and done, I was here in the police station, well and truly trapped in this *they*, and Julien was probably nonchalantly getting on with his reading behind the protective storm-window of the café, flicking through his book which, to quote him, *gave him the necessary serenity of mind* and in which he re-immersed himself whenever he was on night duty, keeping one eye on the screens, so that with one eye on the screens and the other on his book, he could, as he said, observe *human misery* in two different ways – his words. That's what his book was about, apparently, *human misery*, which corresponded exactly, according to him, to what we could see before us, namely people being tossed about on the waves for a bit, then sucked down into the abyss, as he affirmed with a smile, pathetic attempts to struggle against the void, he added, and a general absurdity quite as vast as the sea we were all splashing about in, all the time. He would fish out quotations from this book and share them with us from time to time, because he considered them *relevant to the situation*, whereas it seemed to me that the opposite was true, that in fact they allowed him to *distance himself* from the situation.

I say this, but actually Julien wasn't a bad colleague, for all his affectation of cynicism, and the uneasiness aroused by his remarks, though the director felt he encouraged a negative state of mind among the team. (We don't need philosophers round here, certainly not that kind. Put that book away, please, and do your job. Keep that kind of *entertainment* for your days off, then – pointing over at me – You're having a bad influence on your colleague.)

But striking these philosophical poses didn't make him any less efficient or professional. One day, he confided to me that before joining the Navy he had wanted to be a priest, though I couldn't tell if he was being serious. As it happens, it struck me as funny, the way he revealed this truth – or lie – in the cafeteria where we had breakfast, overlooking the sea, just for a change, as though for all his so-called detachment he was actually sharing a great secret that explained everything. It was funny because I could have shared similar secrets with him, showing that for all my good-little-trooper-look, in my uniform, I was not quite what I seemed either. But I had no interest in telling him my life story, pointing out, for example, that I knew his quotations, too, and could have come up with others that would have been equally relevant to the situation. He wasn't the only person in the monitoring station who knew Latin and Greek.

In any case, if I had been feeling mean I could have told the police inspector (who, as well as feeling I had not done what I should have, also seemed to feel I hadn't used the right expressions for the circumstances) how Julien used these quotations when he was on duty with me, and to what end. For example, I could have told her how most of the time he responded to the distress calls from the migrants on the small boats with the same supposed quotation, accompanied by a fatalistic shrug – which of course they couldn't see but which Julien put on for us, for me – responding to the calls in English with a French quotation, because, in case you don't know, Pascal wrote in French not in English, saying with a shrug of his shoulders, *Vous êtes embarqués,* in a way that implied they should have thought about it earlier, instead of complaining now; it was too late now for a u-turn, saying all that, though I can't describe exactly the tone he said it in.

And as it happened (in the office at the police station, as with every passing minute I was increasingly cast as the fundamental or indeed sole cause of the disaster) one of Julien's stupid quotations popped into my head, one he liked to use to put a shine on his cynicism or conceal his upset. When she asked me what, in my opinion, had caused their boat to sink, why they had ended up there, and why they had been found there next morning, i.e. floating on the sea's surface, this quotation seemed to me to apply to the situation, even to sum up perfectly what I thought, and I declared outloud that 'all of humanity's problems stem from our inability to stay sitting quietly in a room', a phrase which Julien regaled us with on a regular basis and which, inevitably, I knew by heart.

It was a saying which the police inspector appeared, at least, not to understand, or appreciate either, and at first she left a beat, then indicated that she didn't see the connection with what we were talking about, unless, and I quote, such remarks were simply yet again designed to cause a distraction, which she had noticed I was rather inclined to do.

But (as I had to explain to her), it was a way of saying that if their being dead when they could have been alive, or rather could have survived, could be put down to negligence, why focus on the words of the radio operator (me) on that particular night, rather than on what I had or had not done? Wasn't it obvious that, in fact, the negligence, negligence *of all kinds*, went back much further, because, I explained to the police inspector, it was perhaps important to determine *when* the real, actual sinking had begun. It might have been an idea to ask this question, in seeking to *shed light on the matter*, and it might then have become clear that what happened to them was simply, in the end, the outcome of a long process or a long story that had nothing to do with me. I was just the last link in the chain, when it was almost too late. All of which, together with its significance, would have been easily understandable if the single question worth asking had been asked, namely, Why do men, women and children drown every night in the Channel or the Mediterranean? Which, therefore, also amounted to the same thing as asking when this sinking started. In this case, the answer to a question like that was something other than my negligence.

When the sinking started? cried the police inspector. Now what are you on about?

Yes, I confirmed, when the sinking started: that's the real question we need to answer. Because these people were sunk long before they sank. They were washed up well before they drowned, and it's as if the wave simply carried them off when they were already washed up on the shore and halfway drowned in the sand, under plastic bags and tarpaulin, pushed to the sea's edge by a bigger, invisible wave, a wave coming from the land, and they were already half dead by the time they got there, the children like foetuses of straw, the women and men like debris, rubbish, dead but unaware of it, floating on the land for hundreds of kilometres before finally floating on the surface of the sea. Their sinking didn't start in the Channel; it started the moment they left their homes. Maybe they even started to sink the day they got the idea in their heads that everything would be better elsewhere, when they started to want supermarkets and child support, when they heard about Social Security or when a cousin living in London told them you could become a billionaire doing the washing up in a Tamil pop-up. You could say, I repeated, that all their problems stem from their inability to stay sitting quietly in a room.

But it's because they have been turned out of their room, isn't it, or because their room has been destroyed, she said. But then who is drowning them? I asked. Who is banishing them, blowing on them, scattering them across the surface of the earth, and sweeping them towards the sea, where they vanish like dust shaken from the coat tails of humanity. What gigantic storm rises somewhere behind them, what gigantic sweep of a broom in Africa or Bangladesh or Afghanistan? One thing's for sure, I'm not the one holding the broom, sweeping them across the earth's surface and throwing them in the rubbish bin of the Channel. In short, you could ask: Who's asking them to leave? Not me, that's for sure.

Again she interrupted me with a gesture of irritation, placing both hands palm down on either side of the computer, looking me straight in the eye. I was struck at that moment by the really quite astonishing resemblance between her and me, not just the hair pulled back off her face, the straight back, the same tension in her jaw that I have, the slightly pointed nose and beauty spot on her hairline, her sharp, inscrutable face, obstinate, *completely objective*, I thought to myself, but also that way of placing her hands face down on either side of the computer, and above all her expression, which is also *my* expression – I mean my professional expression, the one I put on to stare at screens, check positions, follow lines of travel – which goes with the clenched jaw and especially with my professional voice when responding to idiots panicking and thrashing about in the water. All of which enables me to become exactly *what I should be*, that is, a function, not an individual or a person but a function – about as personal, or individual, as a mathematical unit or a mass-produced tin-opener. If I was behind a counter I would wear exactly the same expression, the appropriate one, a sort of universal expression, and it was as though I felt I was looking at myself, and consequently as though I was questioning myself, as though I was looking at myself in a mirror and saying to myself:

Do you not think that's rather an easy way to…

But again the police inspector was hesitating over the right word and it wasn't difficult to see why, because the terms that should have followed on from the start of this sentence would have seemed like a bad pun, like what immediately sprang into her mind and mine, phrases like *dilute* one's responsibility or even *drown* one's responsibility, which suddenly made for an awful lot of drownings to factor in. (And also, I was waiting for her to produce, as was bound to happen sooner or later, the kind of metaphor that is really just an obscene sort of pun, the kind used by newspapers, militants or political figures when stating emphatically that this issue is about the *sinking of Europe*, or that it's European values that are *foundering* in the Mediterranean, just as I was pretty sure she would sooner or later say that I, too, had *sunk* that night, that it was my moral conscience that had *foundered* and why not – that works too – use the word *perdition*?)

She picked up her sentence where she had left off and added another to the effect that, anyway, maybe it actually was *my* responsibility that was in question and not just that of my department, my colleagues, my superiors, French law, the lack of resources, or human wretchedness or God knows who else (she actually said *God knows who else* and I was pleased to see we were now bringing Him into it) and that in this profession, particularly this profession, what was required, it seemed to her, was as much a sense of responsibility as a sense of initiative or the ability to take decisions.

I just can't figure out, for example, she went on to say, why when the English were insisting you send a patrol boat till they could get there themselves, you said you couldn't do that, claiming it was out on another mission. Do you know why I can't figure it out? she asked me. Because it simply wasn't true.

So back we came to me again, and the idea that the cause of their death was – me.

In other words, not the sea, not migration policy, not the trafficking mafia, not the war in Syria or the famine in Sudan – me. My judgement, to be precise, since she went straight on to ask if I felt I had *assessed the situation correctly*. An error of judgement, then, with them drowning not because their boat was leaking, but because my judgement had a fissure or a hole. I had not assessed the situation correctly, and they were dead. When she laid it out like that it was fairly easy to understand, but I did ask what would have happened if I had assessed the situation correctly. Dead just the same, by the time the rescuers got there, as happened half the time. Unless it was dead *perhaps*, in which case between dead *perhaps* and dead *for sure* there was an irreducible gap that from now on would always stand between me and innocence.

But the exact nature of this error of judgement was not easy to determine, because assessing the situation didn't just involve correctly evaluating what it was possible to do, understanding how best to utilise the resources available, finding the right solution to save these people, with the risk your calculations would be wrong if the waves were actually pushing in the opposite direction, in other words not pushing them into British waters but sending them back into ours, for example, where there are no rescue boats for them, or pushing them into British waters, but with the British patrol boat too far away. In fact, that was what had happened, so where was the error of judgement in that, because my judgement and any rescue effort stops right there, at the line between those two territorial waters, not the other side of it? My judgement has no holes in, no fissures, but it does have boundaries, which correspond exactly to the boundaries of territorial waters, I said. It's that simple.

That wasn't the question, really. What assessing the situation correctly actually meant was understanding that they were in the process of drowning and basically she was asking me if I understood when someone is dying – which was not at all the same kind of error of judgement, of course, and possibly not the same kind of judgement either.

Assessing the situation, however, is exactly what my job requires, and if I couldn't distinguish between someone who *thinks* they're about to drown and someone who actually *is* about to drown, I might as well take a job as a baker, or sell fresh eggs at the market. Because in this job, I said to the police inspector, who was as like me as a pea in the same pod, the crucial thing is assessing a situation, and that's how you learn to sort quickly. Sorting is a significant element of my job, perhaps even the most important.

Sorting, she asked, what does that mean: sorting?

Sorting out what they're saying, their words, when they call you. Not all their words are equal. Because what you also need to realise is that as soon as there's a bit of a high wave, or a bit of a strong gust of wind, and the temperature drops a little, they whip out their phones as though I'm the after-sales service at Darty. And what actually happens is that they take their useless heap of rubber dinghy and the moment they leave the beach they start to panic and remember that they can't swim in water that's eight degrees, or they decide that ten minutes of trying is enough and that for the remainder of the trip we'll be their travel agency.

Now I'm someone who knows the difference between when someone *really* needs assistance, urgent, vital assistance, and when they can wait, because if we only went by the shouting and the trembling in their voices, and the sound of lapping water, every one of them would be top priority. I can tell exactly who to give priority to, not only depending on their own situation but on the situation with the rescuers, what resources we have to hand. But you can't know *everything* either, and besides, especially with these people and that particular vessel, there was another parameter to take into account, which was that they were right on the edge of English waters, and by the time our patrol boat arrived, they would have crossed the line, given the direction and the current of the waves, and indeed that's exactly what did happen, and when that happens it falls to the British coast guards, not ours, mine; it's up to the English to sort it all out and it's the English you need to ask why they didn't manage to save these people who were drowning in *their* waters, and whether, after all, it wasn't actually their *negligence,* their *error of judgement,* whether by any chance it wasn't they who *wrongly assessed the situation*.

They were too far from the small boat, corrected the police inspector, when the French patrol boat was no more than twenty kilometres away, and if someone had really made up their mind to send the patrol boat to the scene – the patrol boat the English actually explicitly asked you to send – there wouldn't be twenty-seven extra dead bodies in the Channel. Do you know how many lives the English saved that night? Let me tell you, she said, with icy fury: ninety-eight, exactly. Does that make you think? Since you clearly take a book-keeping approach to the matter, let's put it like that: ninety-eight lives saved on one side, twenty-seven dead on the other. Looks like you didn't come across the right migrants, unlike them: yours weren't savable I guess, or maybe the others were professional swimmers.

And again I looked out of the window.

There was a brief silence and then, no doubt thinking I was rattled by her remarks she said, Now I'm going to be frank with you. And in order to be frank she felt the need to get up and move away from the desk.

You can try and shift the blame on to the entire rest of the world, but if you're not prepared to admit to an error of judgement, how do you explain that you didn't send the rescue services, didn't inform the English of the likely condition of the dinghy, that you even dissuaded the ship that had spotted them from changing course to go to their aid? Which explanation should I pick for these facts: error of judgement or murderous intent? What am I to conclude, she insisted, that you made a mistake? That you were negligent? Or that you acted with such ill-will, such insensitivity and such indifference to the fate of these people that they died? Or is it all three at once? Which do you prefer?

So I was meant to understand that in fact the distance between doing wrong and wrong-doing was actually not that great, just as it is only one small step from unwillingness to ill-will. And suddenly we were no longer talking about an error of judgement, whatever the nature of that judgement might be, or about a wrong assessment of the situation. The failure was not to be found in the CROSS services, but in me. But not even in me, rather in my capacity to assess the situation and take good decisions: in my soul, so to speak, if such a thing exists. So perhaps the failure was not confined to that particular incident, either, but extended beyond the circumstances of that night. It wasn't just that I slipped up that night, that I'd gone off piste for a few hours, forgetting something everyone else knew or temporarily mislaying something everyone else possessed, my moral conscience or humanity, it was actually the macabre revelation of a failing or anomaly in me that was part of a much longer-term condition. Ultimately what needed to have *light shed* on it was a monster.

As the newspapers continued to talk about the story, and it became clearer that I had not sent the help I should have, that it was not just my error of judgement, my incompetence, but my incomprehensible obstinacy, my professional or quite simply the mechanical coldness of my responses to the heart-rending calls, and above all what really looked like a straightforward refusal to assist people in need of assistance, and this was what had killed these people, I kept on encountering phrases like *moral insensitivity*, *lack of empathy* or straightforward *dehumanisation*.

This time I did wonder by what sign, on me, in me, I might have measured this famous dehumanisation. I guess saying that I had a little girl and that she was the apple of my eye, that I was a good mother who had commendably looked after her when her father had left the conjugal home, and that I looked after my elderly parents – I guess that wasn't enough, since the guards in the concentration camps loved their families too. And to say that I did my work simply and conscientiously wasn't enough, either. Because Eichmann did his work just as conscientiously as me. And if I added that I listen to Schubert, it wouldn't be true, but nor would it be proof of my humanity, either, because the Nazis were fond of Schubert too.

But since *lack of empathy* was an expression that the investigator had also used a few minutes earlier in connection with my way of recounting the facts, I reminded her of what I had said initially, namely that empathy is expressly discouraged and it isn't hard to understand why. Either you save, or you sympathise. Either you ask questions or you act. So, I asked, what would you prefer: that I organise the rescue mission or that I sob down the microphone with them? I'm accused of lacking a soul, but my soul is precisely what I leave in the cloakroom when I get to work, it simply can't fit into my uniform. I pick it up again intact from my locker when I leave. No soul and no convictions on the job; your soul is governed by someone else, I imagine, elsewhere, telling me you *must* save people in danger of drowning, which I do because I'm told to, just as I would save kittens or baby seals. I simply have to be told that's what I must do.

Empathy, I said to the police inspector, is an idiotic luxury indulged in by people who do nothing, and who are moved by the spectacle of suffering. Good for them. But the truth is you can't do both at once. There are people, I suppose, who specialise in being moved by the fate of others, simply by taking an interest in their fate, and I suppose they are necessary and I trust them to tell me what I ought to do; but that's not my strong point, and besides that's not my job. My job, more broadly speaking, is not to take an interest in people's lives or to be moved by their suffering, feigned or real, it's to fish them out of the water when I have to. I don't want to know these people. I don't want anything to do with them, or their lives – I mean their lives up till now, their existence, their story, who they are, what they've done or what they are worth and especially not what drove them to be such fools. All I care about is life stripped bare.

And in fact it's exactly like that, in that state, that we fish them out: as lives stripped bare. Just arms and legs, stiff with cold, trembling backs, stupefied faces, as though they'd only been alive five minutes, with no past (and not much future), no connections, no rights, no nationality. They are nothing, they are no one, no one in particular, even if they have clothes. They are naked bodies that must be wrapped up in gold thermal blankets.

The truth, I said, is that in order to save these people, you simply must not think of them or treat them in any way as single individuals. We save lives, not individuals, and as for knowing whether a life is that of an engineer who has been tortured, or a doctor running away from a war, a man who lost his wife in Sierra Leone, or an abused woman or a child who wants to see Big Ben, I don't give a toss – forgive me for putting it crudely. The migrant who supposedly called me fourteen times could have been a moron who beat his wife, a hopeless case or a bastard, and he's not going to start cleansing his soul just because he's choking to death in water at ten degrees. The point is I don't care. I don't care about his soul, or his history either. I tell him to send me his geolocation; I don't stop to ask him to confess his sins first. In return, I'd appreciate him not asking me to pass him a handkerchief to wipe his eyes or to talk to his wife or his daughter who are in this shitty situation because he's put them in it. That's not my job.

Even though what I was saying was completely obvious, the police inspector looked disconcerted (or alarmed maybe?) and even though she was ten years older, she now seemed younger than me, and muttered, Judging by the recordings, at least, you don't seem to have formed a very clear picture of their situation.

But that's the point, I don't form a picture of their situation, I had to insist, because we're not supposed to see, or create an image. At the start, I had too much imagination and if you have too much imagination you're done for. All the misery of the world can come crashing down on you, it keeps you awake at night. It's the same with their voices: if you let yourself fall for a voice on the other end of the line, it will grab hold of you and drag you in, and before you know it, you find yourself on board their boat with them, trembling with cold and fear, your nose level with the waves, and how will you help them? They try to lure you in; their voices on the telephone are like grappling irons, trying to hook your imagination and tug on it. Their voices are like siren songs; you have to resist and block your ears while you listen. You have to say to yourself: You won't catch me with your words, your weeping, your pleading. Don't try to lure me towards you, don't try to show me your face. I don't need to know your face, I don't want to see it, or the faces of the people round you either. I don't want to picture the little girl next to you. I don't want to see the water seeping in everywhere, or the dinghy deflating. I don't even want to hear the sound of the sea, I don't want to see it. Just give me your geolocation and have done, you'll get your rescue boat. It's not going to help if I'm sitting next to you bailing out, screaming with terror like your wife. If you want me to help you, I need to keep dry. So stop talking to me, stop telling me you're frightened.

But they must talk. And you might think it's the crackling line, losing the signal, the inaudible words, the background noise, that maintains the distance, but the exact opposite is true. It's like their voices are landing directly in your guts without passing through your ears or mind. Then, fortunately, after a while, you realise that you mustn't let yourself be drawn in; you must stay on the shore and not fling yourself stupidly into the water to save them. That or rise to a great height and look down on it all from the sky on the radar screen. From up there the sea becomes just a black, uniform surface, plunged into everlasting and uninterrupted darkness, and all you can see are little luminous dots moving about in fits and starts on motorways that rise and fall, light up, then go dark, little squares and little triangles trailing their orientation segment like the tail of a shooting star, and then disappearing. At this height, at least, there's no risk of seeing their anoraks squashed close together and children vomiting and crying, and it's pretty much what the good Lord must see from up there – the world like a radar screen to him with straight lines, dotted lines and quadrilaterals, except he does nothing, he doesn't send help, he lets them sink, which is pretty much what I did, too. But curiously, when it's the Good Lord, even though – I've been told – he possesses far more resources than the French navy does – no one seems to find that scandalous, though you might say that these poor people, at that moment drifting on the sea at night, are far more in His hands than in mine.

Anyway, after a while you learn to get things in proportion and your imagination naturally runs out of steam, which is a good thing, because that's when you get really good, that is to say, the way you're meant to be. But the people watching from a distance demand that you tear up, as though you'll see the trajectories more clearly with eyes full of tears, to give proof of *humanity*, and also, I guess because I'm a woman as well, I'm meant to display a higher degree of sensitivity, humanity – and why not maternity while we're about it, since as well as all that I have a little girl. I ought to reassure them, cajole, even, why not… why not sing them a lullaby as the sea cradles them before it swallows them? As it happens, I actually did. I said to them, over and over, help is coming…

But it wasn't true.

Yes, it *was* true: the English had been notified and had dispatched a patrol boat. Help was coming, but in the end it didn't come. Now, I can't help that, and let me repeat, that was a problem for the English, because they were in English waters and from that point on it it's nothing to do with me; it's a problem for the English. So what could I say but help is coming? If you think about it, you might even interpret it precisely as a gesture of humanity. It seems to me, when you're in a tight spot it's not only informative but comforting, to believe – if not to know – that the rescue services are coming. At any rate, that's all I can tell them, that and to calm down.

That's just sickening, what you're saying, the police inspector exclaimed. Over and over she said it, sickening, sickening, which isn't really a police kind of word. I couldn't really see what it was doing there. By now she was staring at me in astonishment, as though seeing me for the first time or something, as if she was realising who I was or as if she'd just come up against something she couldn't identify, as though encountering an unknown and completely bewildering species of animal. Maybe, more simply, a madwoman. This she confirmed, in her way, by claiming she did not understand the attitude which, in her view, I had supposedly adopted during the interview. And when I asked her what attitude exactly she meant, she replied, I feel like you're doing your utmost to sink yourself.

She clearly thought I was rather intellectually limited, since she found it necessary to spell out that instead of acknowledging sincerely the negligence clearly indicated by both the facts and the recordings available – such as, for example, the fact that I had not informed the English of the presumed condition of the dinghy and consequently of the true situation of the passengers – when this was perfectly obvious, given that behind the cries and shouting there was no sound of an engine – rather than acknowledging this piece of negligence, which was admittedly heavy with consequences, along with a number of others, I was instead, for reasons she could not understand, adding multiple layers of provocation and bizarre statements, all of which contributed, in a general way, to making me seem particularly repulsive and at the same time virtually incomprehensible. In short, that I was deliberately choosing to present a *thoroughly terrifying* image of myself. Those were her words.

What image? I asked, as a genuine question.

A monster, she said.

I smiled.

She sighed. I don't know why that makes you smile. And to be honest I'd rather not know. Is it a puerile reflex or are you really in some completely other moral world?

There are only two possible explanations, as far as I can see, each as damning as the other. Either your attitude stems from a particularly stupid line of reasoning, by virtue of which, in an attempt to escape the obvious liabilities and avoid acknowledging anything whatsoever, you are getting yourself into a far more serious liability: or else you are quite consciously trying to sink yourself (the unfortunate term she used). In other words, either a ludicrous and counter-productive logic or a suicidal logic. But in the latter case, make no mistake, I have absolutely no desire to follow you down that path. I am not the voice of your conscience and have no intention of saying out loud what it is trying to accuse you of in silence. That's between you and yourself.

So what did she think she was doing, exactly? Because it really felt to me as though she had overstepped the strict boundaries of a judicial investigation a while back and was now engaged in what looked very much like a moral assessment of my behaviour, of my character, even. Though it didn't bother me in the least that we had got into this territory.

In spite of everything, her remark made me think. Not in the way she would have liked, of course, but in a more general, and actually more interesting way, because I began to wonder at this point if one could conceivably imagine any other kind of logic, as she expressed it, apart from those two, when it came to justifying one's acts, or indeed one's words, in other people's eyes or in one's own. It was either ludicrous, as she put it clumsily, or suicidal. But whatever the logic, the result was the same: sinking, as she again put it, because it's precisely when you're trying to wriggle out of something that you start sinking, unless you're actively willing it. In the end, the only thing you succeed in saying is *I'm guilty*, whether you refuse to say it or you're actually trying hard to say it. You say it when you say it and you also say it when you're saying its opposite.

In other words, I thought, you can never, ever say I am innocent, and even less prove it; that kind of illusion is fine for judicial procedures, probably even necessary, but all it indicates is that the possibility of proving one's innocence is conditional on the existence of a presumption of innocence. Therefore, I established logically, it's circular, completely circular, and the whole issue seemed blindingly obvious to me. One can only prove one's innocence to the degree to which one has assumed one is innocent to start with. You end up where you started, having proved nothing, because it amounts absurdly to providing proof of an axiom on which the very possibility of providing proof depends. But the fact is that no one is prepared to admit it's an illusion, because the illusion hides the exact opposite, namely that everyone is guilty.

Now, while I was thinking through this significant problem and, as a result, remaining silent, staring out of the window, she again assumed I had no interest in the question. You don't care, do you, she said, about what I've just said? From which she felt it necessary to conclude: You're still not ready to face reality, while for my part I was thinking Circular, circular.

Right, let me show you them, she exclaimed in a sudden ridiculous outburst, let me describe them to you, she repeated, this time with an emphasis I found distasteful. There they were in the middle of the night, in water at ten degrees, adrift with a broken motor, helpless in the grip of the current, women, a little ten-year-old girl, twenty-nine of them in a dinghy filling up with water, miles out to sea, no horizon, no light, nothing and no one, the swell, the water rising, reaching their ankles, their shins, their legs, pouring in, the dinghy deflating, freezing cold, soaking wet, terrified, and quite simply, realising they were going to die, to drown. Are you getting the picture?

And there's something else I could show you. Around half four in the morning, a ship spotted them. At that hour they must have already been in the water, the dinghy broken apart, in other words a desperate situation, they must have been clinging to life by their fingernails, some of them no doubt dead. They cannot have failed to see that boat. Can you imagine what they must have thought at that moment, what they must have hoped for? And when on the basis of your judgement the ship set off again without coming to their assistance, and they saw it moving off, abandoning them to their fate, can you maybe imagine what despair they must have felt?

And probably she was expecting me to react to all this unseemly pathos, but again I chose to remain silent, and she misinterpreted my silence, thinking I had been affected by her words. At which she decided to ram her point home, as they say.

Still can't picture it? she asked, sarcastically. But perhaps there is one thing you can imagine. Between the first call for help on the recording and the last, more than three hours elapsed. It took them three, four hours to drown. You can't imagine those hours either? I won't even bother asking, even though it is the object of this investigation how in three hours no one could be bothered to save them, it's not as though they were in the middle of the Pacific Ocean as far as I'm aware, they were on a strip of sea that takes ninety minutes at most to cross in a ferry, I'm simply asking you, can you actually not imagine what they went through in those three hours, what it feels like to spend three hours watching yourself die. And I'm not asking you for my sake, she felt obliged to add, but for yours, because if you can't get your head around that, you need to be asking yourself some questions: it doesn't take much imagination to be a moral person.

But you just find that annoying: it's annoying because they keep on and on calling you over those three hours, instead of just putting up with it. It's annoying when they beg for help, when they repeat fourteen times over that they're going to die and you've got to do something. I can quite see that must be annoying – idiots saying the same thing a thousand times over like children, as if they were misunderstanding, instead of taking a step back, calming down and sinking in silence.

Now actually she had described nothing at all and it didn't help me to picture their faces or their anoraks. At best, what I saw was the bodies floating on her desk, still, which she pushed away every now and then with her hand. So, yes, it was annoying, I replied calmly, yes, it is annoying when they call you fifteen times to repeat exactly what you understood perfectly well the first time and when you've repeated exactly the same thing yourself fifteen times to them, but they don't seem to have understood, you don't need to be sarcastic about it. People who continue to call for help while you're busy helping them – even firefighters find that annoying, and firefighters usually end up telling them to calm down or even shut up and let them get on with their job. Would you call them inhuman? And it's also annoying because it happens night after night and maybe they could give that a second thought before they put their lousy nutshells in the sea at sunset. So I don't mind trying to fix their immediate situation, but don't ask me to imagine their distress as well, or to do it with a happy heart, because, let me say it once again, heart and soul simply don't come into it.

So what exactly was I being judged for? My tone of voice? My choice of words? Or the degree of my inhumanity? Because if it's that, could someone please tell me what scale of measurement was being used. Which words, what tone of voice set me beyond the pale of humanity? Was I being judged on my real or supposed intentions, my degree of motivation – though judging by hidden intentions or secret motivations is downright dangerous, not just demoralising, given what happened? So was I going to be incriminated because I didn't seem to be helping out willingly? Surely no one was saying I killed them because I was annoyed, if that's what it amounts to in the end. What sent them to the bottom wasn't my so-called errors of judgement, or my so-called lack of humanity or my so-called incapacity to get my head round their suffering. It wasn't my moral insensitivity that let the air out of their dinghy and cut a hole in the floor, to my knowledge, and wasn't my moral failure but a failure of the motor that threw them off course. Nor was it my so-called inappropriate remarks that pressed down on their heads when the water was up to their necks. They are dead because they put themselves in mortal danger, and they put themselves in mortal danger because instead of sitting in their rooms they left, and it wasn't me that asked them to leave.

It was difficult to say or think otherwise, I felt, but she wasn't prepared to give up. She decided to return to more direct matters, which, to be honest, puzzled me, too. One thing in particular. *Why did you lie?* she asked, because she was fixated on this so-called lie.

Not the one I'd admitted to, where I said that the rescue services were heading their way when they weren't – a lie I put to them with mounting irritation as their calls became more and more insistent. Rather the one which may or may not have been an outright lie – I couldn't quite remember – when I told the English that it wasn't possible to send our patrol boat because it was busy on another mission. This didn't feature clearly in either the written report of the night's operations or in my own memory.

Why had I said that? And what would I have had to lose in any case, in sending the patrol boat which was not all that far away? It was not quite clear. It can't have been because I was worried about infringing maritime law, seeing as the English themselves had requested it, and it's something that happens all the time, in one direction or another. More likely I thought that the English would just have to work something out because by this point they weren't our migrants, they were their migrants. In fact, these people, who were neither French nor English, were nonetheless more English than French now. I must have thought they were no longer our concern and we needed to keep back our resources for what was happening at our end, because, after all, there were dozens of similar boats out that night, no doubt with their cargo of women and children, since the weather was favourable and the sea was calm, and as soon as the weather is calm everyone rushes out at once. But the sea is never really calm, it's just more secretive and shifty and it would be equally happy to gobble them up given half a chance, and for that reason it made sense for us to reserve our resources for those in French waters, for our migrants, if you like, though migrants don't belong to anyone and that's the whole problem, and particularly theirs. So could it really be said, technically, that I had lied?

I was trying to catch the thread of my thought, but couldn't find it. Obliged once again to go back over the sequence of my actions, I had the strange sense that, on the one hand, I could justify everything; that broadly speaking these acts were coherent, their order logical, the decisions rational and therefore virtually irreproachable, but that on the other, deep down and underneath these explanations and justifications lay something aberrant and inexplicable. A kind of foundation on which everything rested but which was itself elusive. So I needed to try and remember my *state of mind*, not my qualms of conscience, since I had none, but my state of mind which alone could account for my actions and the words on the recordings. But the effort was not just a strain, it was also fruitless. I couldn't find my way back to my mood back then, maybe because the way back was cluttered with a whole load of feelings, judgements, words, things I had read, things that had been said, comments, interpretations. The little I could grasp of myself by stepping over all that and trying to think back to the situation, as though I was re-living it, seemed aberrant to me, too.

All I could access was a kind of lethargy. An absence, a loss of consciousness, as though none of it was true, not completely. And I got stuck at that point, unable to advance, or shed any *further light*, unless perhaps by describing the prevailing atmosphere in the operations room.

She said, Yes, describe the atmosphere to me, and I expect she probably thought that the atmosphere of the operations room, nocturnal and muffled, diligent but also incredibly enclosed, must have encouraged a certain distancing from reality, the real world filtered through the screens, software and radio communications, warded off by the huge, hermetically sealed bay windows beyond which there were only the two dimensions of a darkly painted canvas.

So I described the operations room as she asked, our balcony looking out over the sea and the way the darkness quickly closes over the useless beam of light, the two traffic surveillance posts, the rescue pod where I took the distress alerts with Julien, the screens, the PCs, the printers, the insect-like noise of fingers tapping on keys, the soft rolling of the chairs across the floor, the radio signals from ships that seem to come from the sea bed, the blue uniforms and white shirts, the studious, library-like atmosphere, faces lit up by the blue glow of the screens – and, of course, none of that explained anything at all. It did not represent my state of mind; not one of my thoughts, impressions or reflections could be flushed out of a corner of my desk, or from one of the files in the cupboard, or the surface of my screens. So,

I had to say No, I can't think of anything. I don't know where I've put my state of mind, and I can't find it now.

Ultimately the conversation – or the interview, I'm not sure what to call it – got us nowhere. We both realised that it had just taken us round in circles, and in any case, due to its sinuous nature, there seemed to be not the slightest possibility of making progress, contrary perhaps to what the police inspector had hoped for. There was no point pursuing this ridiculous, useless interview.

I was also becoming increasingly absorbed in what was happening outside the police station window, even while I was responding to her questions – which in any case seemed to me always to be the same question, and I felt the interminable meandering of her interrogation had so little to do with me. (Why, after all, call what was clearly an interrogation a conversation, even if it was obvious to me she really wasn't conducting the interrogation in line with the normal rules; she wasn't exactly talking like a police inspector should. It is, after all, a military role, as mine is, and the military don't use those expressions or, more generally, those protocols. She should have simply stuck to the facts and maintained a scrupulous distance, which she definitely didn't. Obviously I'm less experienced, but I wouldn't have conducted the interrogation that way, asked those questions, and even if the most important question was establishing whether there had or had not been a failure to help a person or persons in danger, I certainly wouldn't have wandered off into absurd moral problems, clumsily presented, or into making judgements or implicit accusations, all of which considerably exceeded the limits of her authority, so that I wondered whether, in spite of what she had said, she might be trying to play the role of my conscience, while exploiting her resemblance to me, which cannot have escaped her.)

It had so little to do with me, as I said, that after a while I simply forgot about the actual police station and at moments began to feel as if I was at home, or on the beach after my morning run when, for example, I sit for a few minutes on the rocks and watch the sea before going back the way I've come. I was no longer looking at the construction site and site workers through the window… (Would you mind looking me in the eye when you answer my questions? the police inspector snapped, in a school-mistressy voice) but rather at the black-headed and herring gulls, and the insipid, bulging, surly sea, eternally churning over some unfathomable grievance or recrimination.

But she was still determined to continue, to keep on with the interview or interrogation, even when I told her I saw no further point or sense in the conversation (I said conversation, not interrogation), since she now had all the necessary elements for her enquiry, and there was nothing else I could add to it. This also meant that I harboured no illusions as to her judgement or the conclusions of the enquiry, though she pretended to adopt a more understanding (I was going to use the term *empathetic*) position, mentioning what she called my youthfulness, considering the responsibilities I had to confront every day in this job. A heavy load, apparently, for my fragile frame.

By this means she sought, casually, to get a foot in the door of my private life – this being the new direction she was trying to lead the conversation in, maybe to find out how inhumanity develops while no one is looking. Since I understood that although she was now trying to learn who I was by direct, sometimes indirect questioning, it was not because she wanted to know more about the life of a naval officer, and certainly not because she wanted to build up a closer, more trusting relationship, but to try and get a picture of what kind of monster was capable of doing or saying those things – an ordinary monster, born of ordinary life. And why not clear up a few edifying riddles while she was about it, like how could someone love and cherish their small daughter and be totally unconcerned about the fate of drowning people, or how could they claim to be doing their job in a professional manner while completely losing sight of the most elementary human values.

From now on she seemed to feel that what had happened to these people was directly linked to what had passed through my mind that night or, to be exact, what had *not* passed through my mind, as though I had suddenly been seized with a sudden *inexplicable lapse in concentration*...

(This was indicated, as she constantly pointed out, by the fact that I had not, according to her, *realised* what was at stake; that I did not seem to have taken it sufficiently seriously; that I hadn't grasped, or had insufficiently grasped, the *reality* of the situation; as though from the top of the cliff where I sat, keeping vigil, high up, far off and – above all – safe in my little bubble, this reality – people drowning – was just a game, as though I'd watched it as you might watch floods in Pakistan on the TV, while preparing the evening meal. And also as though, now that I was sitting in her office at the police station, mostly preoccupied with watching workmen on the building site opposite and the gulls over the beach where I go running, I was still submerged in this absentmindedness and that, whatever I might say to the contrary, I still hadn't *realised*, I still hadn't really grasped the reality of the situation.)

...and that the only possible explanation for my inexplicable lapse of concentration must lie somewhere in my private life, in the events of my private life, quite possibly in my character or personality or even, while we were at it, in some childhood trauma (though she would find not the least trace in my early life of a shipwreck) which would finally explain why I appeared to feel indifferent, at one fateful moment, to the life and death of twenty-nine people...

(She was maybe convinced that my personality would prove to be not that of a classic dim-witted member of the armed forces, but of a mindless idiot who could no longer distinguish between reality and what comes up on her Instagram feed – the umpteenth iteration of the irresponsible dumb babe, plugged into a constant stream of social media, bottle-fed reality TV; someone who measures reality by the yardstick of celebrity; for whom fashion week is the one and only important event of the year; who has no idea what a human life consists of, and who, unbeknown to herself, would rather, as someone or other said, see the whole world destroyed than break a fingernail. In short, the archetype of witless humanity who has had no need of a bureaucracy to shape her, having been mass-produced, naturally and seamlessly, by present day moral and cultural conditions.)

...Because to say, as I had probably done at the outset, but I couldn't exactly remember, that I was naturally very sorry they had died, in fact it was tragic, that I fully understood the gravity of the situation etc. – and I think I adopted an appropriate facial expression in saying it – none of that was sufficient to bring me back into the fold of moral beings, and it certainly didn't change the fact that on that night at least, I was apparently not sorry at all and had precisely *failed* to understand the gravity of the situation, etc.

But while she was busy grilling me about my daughter, my parents, my ex, Eric, and how I had found my vocation as a coast guard, while she was hoping perhaps to identify the *primary cause* of all that, the origin of the monster of banality, I did wonder if it was really so extraordinary, this *incomprehensible absentmindedness* as she chose to call it, probably thinking this was a charitable interpretation. Was I really alone in being occasionally subject to such absentmindedness, the kind that might not actually lead us to be indifferent to other people's lives and deaths, but possibly, if I can put it this way, to a failure to accord them *due weight*, which is simply the weight of reality? What she called absentmindedness seemed to me so unremarkable, so common, and so universal – indeed the basis of everyday life – that one could only conclude that all of us are monsters, that is to say, none of us is.

So, instead of asking the true question, and arriving at this true conclusion, which probably was too painful for her – as for everyone – to contemplate, she asked me how I managed to juggle my professional and family life, someone to look after Léa when I had all-night shifts, and sometimes even all-week shifts. That can't be easy, she said, with fake concern. Do her grandparents have her then? And wasn't it really hard for me and for my daughter, she asked. Usually people are either single or childless; the demands of the job don't leave much time for life. And of course it must be harder still since your partner, Léa's father, left. And had the split with Léa's father been difficult? And what had my relationship with him been since? Indeed, what it had been like before? Not too good, presumably, since in the end I had *asked him to leave.* (Does that phrase ring any bells, she asked craftily.) Maybe a drink problem, the kind of hobby that tends to deaden the moral sense. But no, sorry, that's more Julien's thing, and while we're on the subject, how about my relationship with my parents, or the question of my vocation – why I chose the challenging job of sea traffic controller – my commitment to helping others, you might say, as expressed in my spectacular disengagement at the crucial moment. Of course, I had no wish whatsoever to go into these details, which were completely irrelevant, and which only seem essential when police officers start acting like psychoanalysts or judges. But all the same, to put an end to these unwelcome intrusions, I said: One Sunday a month, at least, as well as the times when I pick up Léa from their house after I've been on a shift, I have lunch with my parents, and after lunch there is always a moment, every single time, when my father pats my hand with a happy smile and murmurs: My little girl saves lives.

I don't know who he's saying it to, since there are only four of us sitting at the table – my mother, my daughter, him and me – maybe to my mother, but she already knows, to my daughter, but she has already left the table and is playing in the room next door. Maybe he's saying it to a person or to people unseen, or to the Good Lord, who he's just been with at mass, making God his witness almost, or commending me to Him. Or maybe just to himself. It might look like pride, but it's more like perplexed admiration, as if it was a great mystery, almost the polar opposite of the mystery of evil, the mystery of goodness, something beyond him, something inexplicable.

I have to tell him that a sea controller isn't the same as a life guard, that the Messiah, to my knowledge, doesn't wear a naval officer's uniform, but it makes no difference. My mother smiles and she and I get up and clear the table, while my father sinks deeper into perplexed admiration and I try not to let my hand rest on the tablecloth at that moment, so he can't seize hold of it; I had begun to find this repetitive monthly scenario intolerable. I begin clearing the table the moment he's about to trot out his immortal phrase, the moment he turns his weepy eyes on me, but he nearly always manages to seize my hand, and even if he can't seize it or catch my eye, as long I'm still in the room, his eyes will settle on some other thing, far beyond the dining table – the plates, the knives and forks, the soup tureen – diving deep down into the world of ideas, the world of good and evil, which is where he finds the phrase I have found intolerable for many years now.

At least from now on, at the end of the meal he'll be able to say, with his sentimental smile: My daughter did not save lives. Which will make a change, I said.

—

Though I didn't actually say that, I just thought it,

because it's no business of a police officer, and she should just stick to her job, which was to interview as part of a judicial enquiry, no more than that. If she wanted to be a priest, sorry, not possible, and if she wanted to be a psychoanalyst, she should have trained as one. But what interested her, it seemed, was finding out who I was, as if the mystery lay there, and the key to the mystery, too, and that discovering who I was would also give her a superb overview of the problem of evil. Clearly the person I was, or that I was reckoned to be, posed a problem for her. Something about the whole package clearly didn't add up. For example, she was astonished by my way of talking, not just by the substance of my replies, but a way of talking, she admitted, that she didn't expect from a naval officer. I didn't know how she thought a naval officer was supposed to talk, and it seemed to me she didn't talk like a police inspector either.

My vocabulary was unusual, she said (she should have been asking herself if it was inappropriate), so what was my social background, and what studies had I done besides the ones that had brought me to a lookout-station? And what did I do for pleasure other than run myself into the ground on the beach in the early morning, because obviously I wouldn't be saying what I was saying if I were a normal naval officer. (Is a naval officer who reads Pascal while they're on duty more normal?)

Of course, my replies to these questions were evasive and meagre, not only because they seemed irrelevant to me and none of her business, but because her line of questioning seemed to me stupid and naïve – characteristic of a too common determination to seek psychological, even pathological explanations for everything. This approach explains nothing of what is essential, and only makes things more incomprehensible still, though it stops you having to address difficult problems. I wondered where this inept investigation would lead us, as we strayed ever further from the matter in hand. I suppose, to give her the full picture, I should have described the inside of my house (maybe I had photos of migrants on the walls with targets painted on them), told her what songs I sang to my daughter at bedtime, described the little front garden, my taste for salted butter and where I take Léa on holiday – to which the answer is, as far away as possible from the sea.

Sensing my reluctance to go down that road, she ended up implying, with increasingly fake sympathy, that, after all, she was for sure there to help me confront what had happened… (You really don't look very well, she even dared say. And: You look like you're at breaking point. Of course, I had to smile at this expression because not only my job but even my physical and topographical situation, the place where I do my job, was literally *at breaking point,* watching the waves break on the shore, *without getting wet*. This whole episode, a tale of word play, expressions which may or may not apply literally – extended metaphors, as we learned to say at college – this whole episode: words on the page, words in your mouth) …As if I had come to see her because I was haunted by the episode, and couldn't sleep…

(Every now and then she interrupted my remarks, to which, I should add, she had at one point applied the word *loony*. She interrupted or punctuated my *loony* remarks with comments of her own, made for her benefit or my benefit, or God knows who else's.

She said, for example: I get the feeling those twenty-nine people weren't the only ones who sank that night – which I found quite offensive but didn't take her up on, as well as other remarks in the same vein, some incomprehensible, some fake-caring or concerned, and some just downright hurtful and inept)

...as though I felt personally responsible for the death of twenty-seven people, in other words as though I had finally come round to thinking that it was me that asked them leave, told all twenty-nine of them to sail off into the middle of the Channel one winter's night in a rotting dinghy with a one in five chance they'd make it. As though I'd come to her for relief from my tortured conscience, seeking absolution or even a penance that would finally free my conscience from remorse, cleanse my conscience, my soul, from this stain that plagued me (which was perhaps what, in her view explained the *surprising aggressiveness* of some of my responses)... as though I had turned up here in her office rather than hang myself in my garage.

So, sometimes during the course of our exchanges she came over as harsh and cutting (as when she insinuated that I had lied about our patrol boat supposedly being busy on another mission); sometimes she pretended to want to help me by clearly establishing the facts, or by alluding to the role of others, Julien, for example, the other teams, my director, the extent of my brief...

(And also, could it not be said that when I asked for instructions, when the duty officer was informed, when the information was circulated in the station, *they* told me: Take your time on that one, let them stew in it for a bit; it will teach them a lesson. Did *they* perhaps say: That will make them think again? Or was it just me that thought that? And *who* was it added: That will chill them out a bit when in fact it was the cold that did for them? I couldn't remember)

...of my powers, the problems with communication and transmission of information. Sometimes I was a small cog in a machine that had malfunctioned – maybe myself even a victim of a machine that ends up *erasing the human aspect* – that was the expression she used at one point – or, maybe not a victim, more like a product of the machine which, you could say, doesn't erase the human aspect but mechanically *produces* inhumanity, manufactures, always on a small scale but with global distribution, something inhuman within humanity, so I too became a kind of machine, or something between a machine and a human. Sometimes I was the wrecker, the heartless woman, the executor of orders with no moral conscience, who asks herself no questions – or fails to ask the fundamental questions you're meant to ask – who completely loses sight of all basic values, as if it was *me* that had gone astray, without moral compass, rudderless, no guiding lights. In the end, it was a fine distinction: I was a woman who, driven by evil intent, had knowingly let these people die – and she gave me a look like the judge at the gates of heaven and hell, pitiless, weighing my soul in the balance before consigning it to eternal torment.

(And because of the irksome resemblance between our facial features, I had the inescapable impression that I was the one sitting in judgement and was summoning myself to the weighing-up of souls or some such final examination at the gates of Saint Peter, before she directed me, or I directed myself, down to the basement)

Between these two, what with questions I've since forgotten or gave up listening to, and answers which, as we went on, I made increasingly laconic, with the uncomfortable feeling that I was repeating the same thing over and over, I felt I was circling round and round the deflated dinghy, equidistant from the roles of victim and executioner, between amoral passivity and culpable intent. I saw myself sent back to my earlier lookout post on the top of the cliffs, with its stunning view of the Migrant Tragedy, contemplating the storm and the shipwreck from the windows of my station, shielded from the wind, shielded from feelings, indifferent, no, worse than that: getting secret pleasure from the spectacle, perhaps, glad to be there at my post, and not suffering the pitiful death throes of the reckless, contentedly murmuring *Suave mari magno…*

In actual fact, she wasn't interested. The truth is she didn't know what *they* (or she) had to reproach me with: what I had done, not done, said, not said, what I was guilty of: if it was my incompetence or my inhumanity that was in question, under the heading of failure to assist a person in danger…

(In actual fact *I* could have enlightened her, told her what she was getting at, unconsciously, what she was grappling for, and of what, ultimately, I was being accused, not by a judge, not by the police, or examining magistrates, but by everyone, because I hadn't needed to sit through an hour's interview – conversation, interrogation – to figure that out and understand it. I already knew that when I came into the office. I knew in the car on the way to Cherbourg. I'd known for weeks: it was not about an error of judgement or understanding, nor a failure to do something, not even a failure to assist a person in danger, but about *what I had said*. Not my actions, but my words, my remarks, my asides, those few phrases I should not have said, and onto which you could pin the true cause of their deaths. And even more trivial than those few phrases, it was about my tone of voice, its utter baseness, since it was my baseness, and my lack of all moral sense that had brought about their deaths)

And she seemed to have even less idea what I *should* have done – dive into the water myself to save them, maybe? Or, why not, sing 'Nearer My God To Thee' down the radio? Explain how to re-inflate their dinghy, or simply picture their faces clearly, imagine their lives, summon them up, one by one, all twenty-nine of them: their countries of origin, their reasons, one person's journey, another's face, the house or field or relatives of a third, the little girl's anorak, her mother's shoes, and weep, weep for their wretchedness and the drowning of their dreams, weep with them and for them, which most certainly would not have saved them, but at least, apparently, would have saved me, would have saved my soul.

II

They had to wait till nightfall to put the boat in the water, a wide, semi-rigid Zodiac, six metres long, with a flimsy deck and a spluttering outboard. They didn't know each other, or hardly. Some had come via Turkey or the Balkans and had possibly never seen the sea, some had already made the dangerous voyage across the Mediterranean. They had squatted around Calais; most of them were Kurds, a few Africans. There were two women and a little girl. They shuffled around on the edge of the dunes without looking at each other, hardly spoke. Then the signal came and they moved forward on the beach. To their left, further down the coast, another group was creeping towards another dinghy.

The sea was calm, almost silent, barely visible in the darkness. Scraping the shore with a lazy movement, it breathed in the distance, darker even than the night. The great sleeping mass of it seemed enormous. They shivered a little. It was November.

Almost no wind, the sea smooth, the sky thick and low, no stars. The dinghy struggled, it couldn't gain speed; the outboard was low in the water, as though bogged down in the thick, heavy substance of the sea being thrown up in chunks by the propeller. It was obvious there were too many of them, and they didn't dare move in case a slight adjustment caused the whole thing to capsize. The deck was sticky, damp with briny pools of water. Some of them were piled up on it, half-lying or crouching; most sat on the buoyancy tubes on either side, trying to spread themselves out evenly to balance the boat, without falling overboard themselves. Most had got hold of a life jacket, others had wrapped the inner tube of a tyre around themselves, some had only an anorak or sweatshirt. Occasionally, they took a quick look back at the coast they had left behind, visible only as distant, twinkling, vanishing lights, a greenish, waning halo. Ahead of them there was no horizon. They had been shown which direction to go in, but it was a useless, futile gesture: out ahead, straight on.

The traffickers knew nothing. They didn't care, they had never made the crossing, they had never been to sea. They went straight back to the camps, or somewhere else, in their cars.

Zipped up in his anorak, his face almost completely hidden by the hood, the young man had positioned himself at the front of the boat, tacitly assuming the job of guide, and with the help of his mobile was trying to figure out if they were going in a straight line. At the other end, right at the back, another man had his hand on the motor and steered.

They exchanged a few brief words, but the noise of the engine drowned them out. Bent over, hunched, occasionally looking up, they headed into the sea wind. The further out to sea they got, the less people spoke. Though the water was calm, the boat struck hard, the sides vibrated, but it didn't progress. Low in the boat the brief glow of a mobile lit up a hooded face before it plunged back into darkness. The little girl was sick, as were the others sitting on the floor of the dinghy, unable to see anything, taking the impact of every wave. But they were at last advancing and soon they could see the glowing constellations of cargo ships moving slowly across the sea; their barely distinct shapes seemed huge to them; they must cross their wake without getting caught in the backwash. Beyond, it was impossible to make out the English coast; it was too far away. They advanced blindly, in a straight line as far as they could tell, but there was nothing to guide them, no course to follow and the mobile network was cutting out. The GPS was freezing; it was becoming harder to get a signal.

The engine stalled a first time and the dinghy almost immediately came to a standstill, with no thrust or energy, heavy, bogged down. A brutal silence fell, the weak swell beating at its sides. It wasn't a fuel problem, two or three of them together tried to restart it. Once, twice, and it came back to life in a sickening cloud of fumes. But again, because it was too heavy, the engine raced and the dinghy struggled to move forward. At last it picked up a bit of speed; they listened anxiously to the sounds from the engine. Then they ceased to be able to see anything at all; even the monstrous, well-lit shapes of the tankers had gone. There was nothing but empty blackness, the obsessive repetitive rhythm of the waves, the vastness of it all. They no longer dared even speak, as though they were riding on the back of a giant, somnolent beast and the crucial thing was not to wake it, to slip along without it suddenly turning around and grabbing them. They advanced a few hundred metres further, then, after spluttering a bit, the engine stalled again, and this time would not restart. Out of power, the boat was now being tossed about, starting to drift, pushed by the weak but invincible waves. They were done for. They began shouting.

Once they realised they would not be able to restart the engine, they wondered what to do. Their disappointment at having failed – they could see they would not be able to make it without help – was mixed with a vague sense of anxiety. They were cold; there was nothing they could do but ask for help. They talked among themselves, tried to understand each other. They could feel that every movement they made threatened to destabilise the dinghy or compromise the surface of its base, which was clearly fragile, but they leaned out to see, anyway. They were looking for a landmark; there was none. Those who still had some charge left in their mobiles wondered what to do. The young man offered to call the rescue service on his. Go ahead, they said. They didn't know if they had already reached English waters. It was pitch black in every direction. They shone the pathetic lights from their torches, but they only lit up a tiny patch of the surface, two metres from the boat, the relentless crests of the waves. These made the vastness around them even more immense.

If the French rescued them they would have to start all over again; they'd be back on the shore; they had no more money to pay traffickers and at best would face stagnating in the Calais mud for months, wandering ghost-like along the railings at the edge of the motorways. They would prefer the English. They thought once they set foot on English soil they might pass through the net and be able to stay there; it seemed many people had. At least they would have got where they wanted.

Urged on by the others, the young man first dialled the number for the British rescuers. After a few minutes someone answered. The young man spoke a bit of English. The engine has failed, he said, the dinghy is drifting. He couldn't work out their position. He said, Help us. He mustn't stay on the line for long, the battery was fading. They told him to call the French rescuers, since they were probably still in French waters and they gave him the number of the CROSS, which the young man had already obtained from the traffickers.

People were growing restless in the dinghy; the call wasn't reassuring, and they had the feeling, now they were at a standstill, that the sea had become choppier; there were troughs, the sea wind was icy. Now and then the man in charge of the engine made a gesture to start it again, but it was a waste of effort, of course. In the endless sky above them, not a single star could be seen.

The first time the young man called the French rescuers, a voice replied saying they couldn't do anything unless they knew where they were; they needed a geolocation via WhatsApp, and from that they would know they were still in French waters. The communication was poor, the signal kept cutting out; around him the voices of the passengers were getting louder and louder, and he couldn't hear everything. He thought he heard them promise help. Now the English and French had both been alerted, there was nothing to be done but wait.

But waiting was the hardest thing. They had gradually calmed down to a kind of gloomy resignation; the muffled roar of the sea had come surging back. Some had returned to their phones, but there was almost no signal where they were now, and they needed to save their batteries. The little girl was pressed against one of the women who was murmuring to her inaudibly. They were trying to get warm, but their clothes were soaked through. The bitter sea wind ruffled the sea. Every so often someone asked the young man when the rescue boat would come, but he didn't know, Soon, he said. Everyone was watching out, listening out, but there was nothing.

Then a murmuring started up; two or three people pointed at something, then a fourth. A rumour went round. People tried to stand up, checking it out, then sat down again carefully. One of them who was sitting on the tube had suddenly given a cry and they realised something was happening. On both sides of the boat the tubes were giving way under their weight. Something was wrong; the dinghy was collapsing, it was starting to fold very slightly in two in the middle. The people sitting in that part were almost at the level of the water. Panic took hold of them. They tried to stand up again, to take their weight off the air cushions, but each movement made the boat list and when they were standing it placed too much weight on the deck. They didn't know what to do.

There was a pump on board and while one of them found the valve and set about working it, they tried with the aid of their torches to see the source of the leak. They listened for a sound, but it was hopeless. At the back of the boat the heavy outboard began to sink. The pump was insufficient; they were exhausting themselves to no purpose.

As the shouting intensified, the young man called the

CROSS again, and the same female voice replied. They must hurry, he urged, the dinghy was broken; it looked like it would sink. The steady, clear voice repeated that the rescuers had been alerted and that for the moment there was nothing more they could do. They must be patient and stay calm, or something like that. The young man insisted that the situation was catastrophic, but couldn't tell if she had heard him.

For a moment they may have thought they were wrong, that though the tubes were sinking lower into the water because of the sustained weight on them, they weren't actually deflating, and they could still wait in relative safety. They quickly realised this hope was misplaced, so they hastily reactivated the pump, but the air chambers continued to deflate. Now at the stern, continuing to get pulled down where the heavy outboard was, the water was starting to reach the deck – tiny little waves spreading, then receding, returning, pooling. They tried to spread themselves around the boat to lighten the load at the back, but then it bowed elsewhere and wherever they put themselves it continued to sink into the water.

They were scanning in all directions, scouring the darkness, unable to see anything but the movement of the waves converging on them and assailing the Zodiac, gripping it like a vice and trying to leap over the inflatable tubes which now offered no resistance or protection. It was impossible to tell in what direction the waves were pushing them, or even if they were still drifting. There was nothing to orient by – the sky above them was completely opaque – and no hope of seeing either coast.

A few people began to bail out with whatever they had, most just with their hands, pushing back the water in a pathetic frenzy. Obstinately it returned, cancelling out their efforts. Before long the entire base of the dinghy was covered, just a few centimetres to start with, but even then they couldn't mop it up, so everyone was forced to spread out along the already semi-deflated tubes, pressing down on them more, and speeding up the process.

The first of them fell into the sea and the sudden brutal shock of cold hit them. With one hand they grabbed hold of the safety ropes along the sides and tried to cling to the boat. No one tried to pull them back on board; there was no point; the boat was sinking and they would all soon end up in the water.

It would not be long now; soon the dinghy would completely fall apart. Since no help was coming, they kept turning to the young man and his mobile; the other mobiles were lost or dead. They insisted, shouting, that he must call back, call them again, the French, the English, whichever. Maybe they'd forgotten or hadn't understood the situation properly. The young man called back. He finally got someone at the other end again, the same voice, both far off and close up, emotionless, always the same replies. You are in English waters, explained the impersonal voice; the English have to come and get you; ask the English. He was saying Help us, we're sinking, Please, he was saying, as the water seized hold of them, one by one. She answered: The rescue services are on their way. The line went dead. A quarter of an hour later he called back. Her replies grew ever more laconic, though he couldn't hear everything, even though they were short. He asked her to repeat what she'd said, and he too repeated, Help us, please. It was useless, but he kept calling back.

The water had submerged the bottom of the dinghy; you couldn't see it now. It had risen to the level of the air cushions and soon only the deflated sleeves would be left. Astride the wreckage, the young man, his mobile rammed to his ear under his hood, surrounded by shouts and cries, watched in horror as the water rose above them and swamped everything.

They couldn't hold on now, and were falling or sliding, one after the other, into the icy water. At first they tried to cling on to what was left of the boat, an end of a rope, the edge of an almost completely deflated tube, the arm of someone still in the boat but who was also entering the water. They were going down. Instinctively they looked for a foothold beneath them, but there was only the vast, bottomless mass of water. The majority couldn't swim; those without a life jacket drowned in a few minutes; two waves, three waves went over their heads and entered their wide-open mouths. The little girl had gone; you could still hear the woman who was with her but she was already a few metres from the boat, moving further away. The sea was absorbing them.

All those who hadn't disappeared in the first few minutes were in the icy water, struggling briefly, then trying to calm their movements and preserve their strength. The random movement of the waves, their invisible strength, split them up from each other, distributing them around the remains of the boat, which was now a shapeless mass. They struggled, arms and legs flailing, to group together, catching hold of a hand here, a hand there; they must stay together, anyone who didn't was lost.

When there was practically nothing left of the boat, and they were all scattered about in the water, the young man made a final call. He said It's finished and soon after the signal was lost amid some indistinct shouting. A few moments later there was nothing left to hold on to; he felt the piece of deck his feet were standing on under the surface disappear, and he slid into the water.

When he first entered the water he couldn't catch his breath; his heart was racing uncontrollably, his breathing completely panicked. Crushed by the cold, shudders running through his body like electric shocks, he kicked his legs, the weight of his shoes dragging him downwards. Absurdly, he brandished the phone above his head to keep it clear of the water, while with the other hand he clung to the useless pouch of the tube, then finally released his grip, and it disappeared. But keeping his hand up in the air became intolerable after a few minutes, the effort sent his heart pounding, and he let it fall, dropping the phone in the water, abandoning it. Though shaking uncontrollably, he concentrated on calming his breathing, slowing his heart. He tried to breathe right from the bottom of his lungs. He must close his mouth, his nose. He must stretch out his arms, release himself bit by bit from the tension contracting and paralysing every one of his muscles.

Gradually things became more stable as he stopped resisting the restless swell. The lifejacket rose up under his armpits, pushing against his chin and head, stressing his neck. The waves buffeted him. Almost at sea level, he could scarcely lift his eyes clear of the waves, or if he did, by pulling his head sharply back with a painful movement, all he could see was blackest night, everywhere. Supported by the life jacket, which he had not pulled tight enough, he let his arms and legs dangle inert, to rest them; the cold gnawed at them and entered his flesh, weighing them down. But the calm he had achieved by a painful effort of concentration was deceptive and unreal, and keeping his head out of the water with his neck stiffened and shoulders rigid with cold, demanded of him constantly renewed efforts, which he summoned up in brief bursts, to tear himself from the slow downward suction of the abyss beneath.

Around him he could make out the shapes of his companions, clustered in little groups. The few movements he was prepared to make, remobilising his cramp-ridden muscles for a few seconds, were aimed at getting closer to them, or at least not losing sight of them. Closest to him, three of them were holding hands, heads barely above their life jackets, bobbing like floats. You could not make out their faces.

Now they were floating, scarcely moving, in the middle of nowhere. All shouts, cries and calls, even words, had died out, and nothing could be heard above the stirring of the waves, a kind of universal silence in which the few voices sounded unreal. The panic had ceased, its astonished commotion replaced by a kind of extended dead time where each of them gradually found a precarious equilibrium in the water, and tried to maintain it with economical movements. The confusion and panic of their thoughts had slowly calmed, and their minds recovered a more normal and regular rhythm, though still steeped in unrelenting, irresistible terror. The threat of the deep black night joined forces with that of the sea, to which they could put up no resistance.

The cold, having cut deep into them, now progressively numbed them; the sea wind whipped the crests of the waves into their faces. The sea carried them, without quite carrying them; you couldn't rely on it, its mass was constantly withdrawing, insufficiently solid, shifting. They held out though, keeping themselves afloat by occasionally making sudden movements with their arms, their legs, abrupt efforts to raise their shoulders, up to their necks in freezing water. The least word uttered above the roar of the sea took their breath away.

In spite of everything, they continued to watch out, as best they could, for the unlikely light of a boat, the right one this time, but there was nothing, and now all they looked for, somewhere on the horizon, above the endlessly lapping waves, was the first glimmer of dawn. That was the only hope they had left, the light of day, as though everything could still change; night could recede without having devoured them, beating a weary retreat and surrendering them to life. So all they could do, since resistance was costly and above all absurd, was float like jetsam, prey to the invisible pull of the currents, tossed about, unresisting, without direction, or intention, their will focussed simply on breathing, economising their strength. Their only task was to breathe.

A moment came, though, when they spotted the garland of lights they had been waiting for and soon they could make out the heavy, spectral silhouette of a cargo ship. It was not the rescue launch they'd been waiting for, and the ship looked a long way off – so far as they could judge the distance in the dark – but it was closer for sure than the tankers and the huge container ships they'd seen go by earlier, when the dinghy was still intact and their main concern was avoiding the lethal backwash of their wakes. And they must at least have believed they had been sighted, so that at best they could they started shouting in that direction, hailing it, waving their arms and exhausting themselves. And they must have thought they'd succeeded, because the boat's fog horn sounded out in the night and a few moments later a lateral search beam came on, casting an intense and unreal light on the waters, groping its way across the surface.

The ship had stopped, they realised, and was waiting in stillness in the night. They had time for hope, still shouting occasionally, without wondering if they could be heard at this distance. The searchlight swept over them, but never fixed on one or another of the groups either dying or dead in the water, so that they didn't know if they had really been located. Though weak already, they exhausted themselves further by waving into the darkness.

But in the end nothing happened. A few long minutes later the searchlight went out, and after a lengthy pause the cargo ship, incomprehensibly, started up again, and slowly turned away from them, abandoning them to their fate. They had to watch helplessly as the enormous structure pulled away into the distance, and soon they could no longer see it, just a few flickering lights, gradually being sucked in by the darkness. They no longer had the strength to curse or swear. The endless night resumed.

They had lost all sense of time now, and of how long it was since the boat had been damaged and started to sink, since they'd been assured that help was coming, or what time it now was, whether dawn was approaching at last. Time both contracted with each tiny effort they made to hold on, to breathe, to resist the biting cold, and at the same time stretched out infinitely. They waited and waited, wondering from the depth of their numbness how long the rescuers might still take to show up. In a kind of mental fog they pictured the boat getting closer and closer; it would soon be there, but now the expectation was represented as the gradual sharpening of the mind as it let go. Each minute that ought to bring them closer to deliverance was a repeat of the previous one, so that each cancelled the last one out, and it was as though the rescue boat never came any closer, but nibbled endlessly away at the billions of infinitesimal little waves without ever reducing the distance, or ever actually getting closer. At certain – increasingly rare – moments, their imaginations suddenly took a leap forward and they pictured themselves being saved, hauled on board, wrapped in blankets, surrounded by people speaking to them. But when they made such efforts, to rewind back through this fictitious period of time in order to gauge their present distance from it, their imaginations almost immediately returned to the succession of minutes which was failing to move time forwards, as if the cog-wheel of time could find no purchase and was spinning in a void.

These were their dying moments, though they didn't quite know it. Bit by bit, all sensation had left their limbs or had fused in one general, low-level sensation of cold, which they scarcely registered any more because their bodies felt like one indistinct mass, a kind of insensate and almost alien block to which they were manacled. Their swollen lips moved and spluttered, their chests were gripped in a vice they could no longer even feel, their throats puffy and compressed, their jaws locked almost rigid. Their faces took on a blue, chalky pallor. There was a ringing in their ears and a kind of continuous stupor overcame them, an irresistible lethargy, which they mistook for calm and the subterranean, indestructible continuity of the vegetative state. In fact they were dying.

The young man, too, was in the grip of a sullen somnolence, which could have been that of exhaustion, or of death, until at long last he and the others saw the sky grow pale and the horizon appear, gradually separating the darkness of the sea from the darkness of the sky, then diluting the blackness with a hazy grey. Before long, they managed to make out birds in the sky, scarcely bigger than dots. The fear that accompanies the night began to fade, and the fear aroused by the bottomless deep above which they were floating also disappeared. The growing light did nothing to warm them, but it roused their spirits slightly, as though they were actually emerging from the abyss and from their ordeal, as though they had survived and their victory was definitive. Some of them, floating on the water, were already dead.

The arrival of day brought no change; hours passed and nothing came. The feeling of having escaped, pulling themselves alive from the night, had encouraged them all to let go of the tension by which they had clung to life, and told them there was no more effort to be made. So they could no longer see, now that a vast fatigue and weariness had come over them, why they must continue to make this effort. An icy hand released the hand or arm of a companion and they floated apart. In spite of the life jacket, each person's head tipped over to one side, water silently entering their mouths, their noses, as they drowned, without even noticing.

Slowly, the young man turned his head. The sea had turned slate grey, just as hostile or indifferent as before. Now you could see the distant shape of the boats, red ones, black ones, passing in a kind of white mist, indifferent as the ones that had gone before, and seeming to belong to another world. The endless, brooding sky loomed like a cliff.

His legs were like stone and he could scarcely move them; his neck was rigid with cramp. Then his breathing began to speed up, without him realising, as if someone was pressing down on his chest to expel the air. He breathed no air in; jolting, his heart began to beat frantically, juddering, slamming up into his throat. He couldn't keep his head up and his chin slumped into the water. He sensed this time that the waters, losing patience, were closing over him.

Something was circling round him, invisible, or scarcely visible, a shawl of mist, winding, coiling about him, unfurling. There was a ringing that wasn't coming from inside his skull, that wasn't in his ears, but was getting closer, now moving away, now closer again, like words scarcely uttered, scarcely audible.

He felt a hand trying to hold him back. He thought, When I get to England I will work in a grocery store. A grocery store, he repeated to himself.

III

I would run about four kilometres eastwards, along the edge of the sea, with the sun rising in front of me, as far as a pile of rocks. When I got there, I'd stop for a bit and sit on the rocks. I'd look at the sea. After that I'd set off again, still in the same direction, for another three kilometres. Then I'd walk back. At that time of day you didn't meet anyone on the beach, usually just mist.

Since I had been officially suspended, I had a lot of time to myself and I could run every morning. I could sit down for longer on the rocks. Léa wouldn't be up yet, she'd still be asleep; when I got back she would only just have woken up and we'd make breakfast. I had nothing to do all day. I could look at the sea. I may not have given much thought to the ongoing legal investigation, but I did think a lot, because that's what happens when you sit and look at the sea: either you think a lot, or you think about nothing, which is probably another way of thinking.

I thought a lot about Léa. I thought, with the sea open wide before me, brown and cloudy, ugly, how little she was, as though the bed in which she still lay sleeping at this hour was nothing but a fragile nut shell. It was an idea I'd had for a long time; it was perhaps one of those ideas you have when you're standing on the shore on an overcast day, because that's when the sea shows its true expression, or rather its least hypocritical aspect, its Hippocratic face.

—

You can't see the harm in this? the police inspector asked me at one point, I seemed to remember, as if I genuinely understood nothing about anything, and she was trying to help me come either to my senses or to something else, a state of greater moral clarity, perhaps. She asked me in the voice you use to speak to children. It wasn't a scandalised question, more like puzzled, almost kindly, really trying to open my eyes, because, according to her, I was keeping them stubbornly closed. There was something I didn't want to see, or rather, recognise. Pointing to the big blue file lying on the desk, in which the elements of the enquiry were accumulating – in other words pointing to the whole story – she repeated, You can't see the harm in all this?

But the question had a bizarre ring to it, as if she was reproaching me for not attending closely enough, or having poor eyesight, or not having a good pair of binoculars to see the harm with. Usually, I am the one with the binoculars – or, so to speak, my microphone is a pair of binoculars, my geolocation screen is a pair of binoculars. Except that you don't see for real, or rather you see more than for real, you see straight through reality – if reality is just what you have before your eyes when you have them wide open, which isn't true reality, or when you stand at the window of the control tower or lighthouse looking out at the sea. I could see true reality much more clearly via a telephone line and the screens than someone with it right under their nose. I see directly *what it is*, not what it looks like. A small boat sinking, a mother screaming, people frozen to the bone and frightened – I see all that much better with my screen and switchboard. I see far better what needs to be seen.

But maybe she was trying to get me to understand that I wouldn't be able to see what the harm was, using all those devices, the instruments, the little series of numbers, the little luminous squares hopping imperceptibly about, carrying thirty people packed so tight together you wondered how they could possibly all fit in one tiny square. You can't see the harm, apparently, using them. So using what then? What instruments should I use?

Actually, though, I completely understood what the harm was and I said, Yes, I see perfectly well the harm in it. Of course I can, the harm is right in front of me. I see it every day and especially every night because the night is its garment, a black garment, with no stars. It's right there under my nose, how could I not see it? Because the harm is the sea. The sea and the night together.

Driving along the Boulogne road from the CROSS, going back to my home and my daughter, the sea was always with me. There *it* lay, the entire length of my journey, on my right, poisoned. There were the terns and the gulls, the greyness, the pallid light, the sea with its guts glutted with women and children. Sometimes, despite the fatigue of the night shift, I had to stop on the way, park the car by the roadside and walk to the edge of the cliff to look at it: the progression of cargo ships, their hypnotic slowness, and *it*, at my feet, in front of me, lifeless, enormous, malign. Universal and monstrous. It's the one thing that never sleeps.

And back home, when I kiss my daughter, I taste salt on her mouth, and see little inflatable boats in her soup, tiny arms emerging from her soup. At least I never hung a mobile in her room, as people often do for children: I would have seen the French navy helicopter circling over my daughter's bed. And on the TV, shouting, spluttering, the living room full of gulls.

Whenever I have a week off, and come running here on the beach, whatever the weather, there *it* is alongside me, pursuing me, watching me while I run, ready to reach out and grab me the second I put a foot wrong, to drag me off and drown me. *It* is waiting, *it* pretends to sleep or be busy doing something else.

I used to love the sea. I remember I loved the sea, because I was born here on the coast, with the sea in my eyes and my nostrils, and the naval base at the end of the road where my school was. It was as if the playground immediately overlooked the dockyard, when there was no dockyard. I didn't just love the boats, the ports, the bobbing of the hulls in the harbour, the sound of the halyards in the wind, navigation, seafood or collecting shells. I loved the sea itself, how it smelled, with its mantle of maritime wind, like its hair almost, a part of it; loved its depth and mass, its absence of form and its sterility – because even the life within it is not *it* – its indifference to everything and above all, its great age. But I never loved what people said about it, all that lyricism and pathos, the poems and the novels, all that mythology and mysticism. Nor what sailors said about it, piling up clichés with ridiculous solemnity, as though they felt they must always be dragging up great truths about the nature of existence which, like anything you pull up out of the water, immediately suffocates and dies a pitiful death.

But I loved the sea. I mean obviously I was aware that it's dangerous, since it's the one thing we haven't managed to tame in thirty thousand years. It's never true, that you can take possession of it, that we've conquered the seas, as they say, because it's not like a land or a field; it's the opposite, its negation. Every sailor fears the sea – unless they're total idiots, in which case they're no sailor. And you can't really love the sea, strictly speaking, if loving means trusting, not fearing, if it means believing that what you love will be good for you, or at least, let's say, wishes you well. So maybe I shouldn't say I loved the sea, because it isn't something you can love.

It causes harm. I can't see how anyone can deny that. But there is a difference between knowing about the power of the sea and fearing it – or with knowing, as I do, that you're dealing with something harmful – the difference between the harm it does and the harm it *is*, and the harm it *is* isn't something many people see. But I saw it from quite a while back.

So, if someone asks me now if I can't see where the harm is, it makes me smile, and I answer: What do you think I have right in front of me day and night? It's not by chance that the sea consumes migrants all night long; it would consume everyone if the land didn't do its best to resist. Every night at my station I can hear the land resisting, digging its heels in, but then succumbing, and the immense sea, black as Hades, opening its maw. Every night we feed that gaping maw, and stuff into it little pieces we've scraped off the edges of the coast, spoonfuls of twenty, thirty poor people – men, women and children – and the monstrous maw gulps it all down, foaming at its mouth. It's the sacrifice the world pours into the mouth of evil, what it has to give it, so everyone else can sleep in peace and it won't devour everything.

Julien said to me once, when we were looking out at it from our observation post, leaving the black screens for a moment to gaze at the even deeper darkness of the night sea, It's the remains of the Flood. And the land we see here – the cliffs, mountains, forests, plains, all of nature – is the ruins of Creation, what remains of the world as it was first created and has since been destroyed. There's nothing left but ruins, the towns are ruins too, and the sea of the Flood is still there, twisting, nibbling, swallowing chunks of the world.

Because we shouldn't believe, he said, we shouldn't be deceived, or let ourselves be hypnotised by the peaceful flow of ships across the ocean – their regularity, order, or rather the illusion of order created by the herds of cargo ships and tankers – proceeding placidly like pachyderms, one meekly following the other; or be misled by our own situation, which makes *contemplatives* of us – those were his words – as well as *employees of the divine bureaucracy*, we shouldn't be taken in by the surface, which deludes us into thinking not only that we have everything under control, but also that the world itself is orderly. He said that these beliefs are reinforced every time we look out at it from our platform, and are unable to see what *underlies* it, beneath the surface, the deep, which is in fact *archaic chaos*, reigned over by Leviathan, not God.

Maybe Julien's religious vocation, long in the past now, supposedly dead and maybe only ever imagined, comes back to him in sudden gusts, and even if the Good Lord has vanished from his field of vision, when he looks at the world he must still see traces of His passage. Julian said Leviathan is the most ancient of creatures, and will probably outlive the Lord God Himself. He never sleeps and neither will he rest till the end of time. And every now and then he turns back and rises to the surface to take a random snap at one of those disorderly and aimless insects. He spoke as though our observation post was a pulpit.

I didn't know if he was saying this for the benefit of the gallery (me), since his tone was comically priest-like, or if that was actually what he saw at that moment, and each time he and I watched the boats going by. I guess it was both. But I'm sure he was right, in his way, and that if an explanation had to be found for my state of mind, that night and every other night I was on duty, the place to look was not in my personality, or the atmosphere of the CROSS (because eventually you do tire of the calls for help from migrants), but rather in my way of looking at the sea, seeing it for what it really is: evil.

But the police inspector said that wasn't what she meant by her question at all. Her voice now sounded as though she was talking not to a child, but to an idiot, or a mad woman. But I'm not mad and I understood perfectly well the meaning of her question and in fact it's she who didn't understand the meaning of the question she was asking me, I said, looking out at the sea, in other words at the *evil*.

But instead of letting me continue, she switched her tone again, and looked at me differently; this time with exasperation and contempt. These mystical flights of fancy, her eyes seemed to say, are just another way of avoiding your responsibilities. Blaming the sea: the most infantile and absurd approach, the ultimate and most pathetic kind of buck-passing, the most desperate, somehow. After that, there's only God to blame, and that was not part of the brief of a police investigation.

But that wasn't the only thing irritating her, because she detected in what I was saying – and had done from the outset – something more repugnant still. Behind what she judged – or at least called – *increasingly improbable justifications* (and at least once, I think, she used the term *sickening*), which she was visibly coming to see as proof not of cowardice so much as of madness, pure and simple, there clearly lay something no less – in fact even *more* – shocking. Is it really *you* we should be feeling sorry for here? she asked me, tucking a strand of hair behind her ear (the way I do, too). Don't you find it somehow obscene, when twenty-seven people have died through your fault, to be feeling sorry for yourself, when surely we should be feeling sorry for them? Because that's exactly what you've been doing, right from the start, that's exactly what you're implying: you're more concerned for yourself than for those men and women (but I was the one being interrogated, I thought, and it was me we were talking about) and also more intent on conveying how much *your* situation, not theirs, was ultimately worthy of pity. And yet that situation might well be described as one in which a person stands safely on the shore while the storm rages out at sea, calmly watching the ship being wrecked.

At this point I wondered why she was suddenly saying 'tu' to me, because she looked so like me with her black hair pulled sharply off her face, and her curt gestures, and her voice with the same intonation as mine. I felt as though I'd merely been talking to myself all this time, and I was the one looking at myself with an expression of weary exasperation, saying, Can you not see there's something indecent about moaning and being so quick to feel sorry for yourself, finding every way possible to avoid your own responsibility? Saying It's sickening, with not a hint of empathy for the victims, always just moaning on about yourself.

And I had to admit that it wasn't her saying all this, but me, and a gust of wind suddenly blew open the window of the police station onto what was quite clearly not a street with, on the far side, a construction site busy with workers, but simply the sea.

I'm not feeling sorry for myself, I said to myself in response to her questions, as I wiped the sand off my trainers, and I'm not trying to arouse your pity. I can't bear pity these days. I'm not looking for any favours either, and if in the end the police in Cherbourg issue me with a summons, as I'm told they will, and if in the end I have to go to the police station to listen to the recordings and hear my voice and my words, as well as the voice and the words of the man who drowned along with the others, if I have to sit and answer the investigator's questions – it was bound to be a she and not a he, a woman police inspector and I was sure she'd look like me too – I won't try to evade my responsibilities, or beg for favours from the judge.

And, I thought, I might even go of my own accord. I'll turn up at the police station in Cherbourg before they summon me. I'll drop Léa off one morning with her grandparents and set off for Cherbourg, four hours drive from Boulogne, stop off once at a motorway service station for an insipid cup of coffee, with people muttering about me behind my back and nodding over at me, get back on the road and end up sitting in front of a desk with a police inspector on the other side, not myself looking at my own image in the mirror, saying to myself, What have you done, my God, what have you done? And it would not be me talking to myself, or to whoever it is inside me, saying over and over: You let them be flushed away, because broadly speaking you didn't really care that much if they lived or died, because in fact these people mean nothing at all to you.

Yes perhaps I will go, in the end, I said to myself, getting up from the rocks, then sitting straight back down again. I will go, and I have no reason to be afraid, because *I am not a criminal*, or a monster, and if I seemed a bit irritated or weary at any point, if I even appeared indifferent to their fate at some point, that doesn't make me a monster. It doesn't mean I am one, or that I've been made into one of those everyday monsters turned out by the dozen by the bureaucratic procedures common to the Office for the Protection of Stateless Persons and Refugees, or County Hall, the CROSS too. As if this little moment of inattention, if I must really admit to it, had put me beyond the pale of humanity for all time. As if, even more than an unforgivable act of culpability, that was the thing I couldn't undo, that moment of inattention, that absence, because I had lost my humanity, because I'd taken my eye off the ball for a moment and would never be able to recover it, when in reality it only lasted a few hours at the worst, and probably only a few minutes in total, a kind of moral sleepwalking for at most a quarter of an hour, leading to a failure on my part to assess the situation and its implications. In other words, I kind of lost sight of what a human life is, with these shedloads of migrants getting dumped in the sea every day. But it's okay. After those few minutes, I completely recovered my humanity. I am not a monster.

So I'm not going to go there and be handcuffed. I'm not going to turn up with a rope round my neck like one of the Burghers of Calais, to acknowledge an imaginary guilt founded on some judgement based on some moral precept or other, not on an article of law, and, really, I have no problem listening to the recordings of that night and hearing my own voice, because it's not the voice of a monster or a criminal on the tape – it's the voice of *all of us.*

And so that the voice of everyone should be clearly heard, I stood up from my rock and went down onto the sand, and I yelled at the top of my voice at the sea spray and the wind scouring the shoreline in little gusts, and since shouting wasn't enough, because given the conditions I couldn't be sure everyone would hear the voice of all of us, I shouted out at the sea: You are in English waters, and then I added, shaping my hands like a megaphone against the hostile cross wind: Help is coming, and then: Calm down, and then again, articulating carefully, syllable by syllable: Calm down, I have told you help is coming.

The only response was the growling of the muddy sea, as though my cries had woken it from restless sleep and it was turning against me saying: Just come a few steps closer and I'll have you.

But had I made my point now? Had I done enough? Had my voice carried far enough to be heard, to be recognised as the voice of all of us? I put my hands back together once more and, taking a deep breath, I yelled: I did not ask you to leave.

And this time I was sure that my voice had carried, in

spite of the wind, flying across the water, skimming the tops of the waves, so fast, so powerful, that the sea could not rise, leap, trap it and gulp it down. It was reaching the open sea, undiminished, flying to where it needed to get to – to that piece of wreckage, floating like a burst balloon, with people in orange jackets scattered all around and a kid clinging to his phone as though it was a safety raft – a ridiculous gesture of defiance which would enrage the sea, make it puff up its grey-white waves – and which, in turn, tried to enrage me, saying: Speak louder. I didn't hear. Try again.

But I stopped shouting and, responding to its taunts, let my arms drop. I gave a shrug of contempt and without raising my voice this time, I said simply: Don't you get it? You will not be saved.

My voice was worn out with shouting. I stood there panting with my hands on my hips. As I turned around I saw, at the far end of the deserted beach, to the east, a figure, scarcely visible because of the mist and the distance – it could have been a rock if it hadn't appeared, slightly but unmistakeably, to move. It was one of those joggers I sometime passed, though usually, as I said, I don't meet many people at that time of day. This brought me back to reality and I decided it was time to set off again. I still had two or three kilometres left to run in this direction before turning back home to make Léa's breakfast. I put my headband back on, did a few stretches, and ran on the spot to warm my muscles up before I set off.

But I stayed where I was.

I was still stamping about on the sand, lifting my knees high, panting loudly, as though building up steam and preparing to shoot off like an arrow, but I was not stepping forward but going round in circles, now to the east, a quarter turn towards the rocks behind me, then another quarter turn to the west and the other end of the beach, and finally another quarter turn to face the sea again, back where I'd started. After a few more of these turns, I stopped, exhausted. I'd started to think about Léa again, in her little bed, and I had the ridiculous feeling, given my present position, that I was the only bulwark – but what a bulwark – between that little bed and the endless surging of the sea opposite; as if simply by thrusting out my chest, I could repel its onslaught. What I was most conscious of was the monstrous menace of the threat weighing down on her, and this image brought my mind back to the previous storms, so to speak, that she and I had had to weather – the difficulty of steering our little craft, as they say, since her father's departure, with me alone at the helm, trying to hold the course, as they say again, and above all, busy bailing out.

What about me, I wondered, watching the absurd, relentless rise and fall of the waves in front of me, what about me? Who came to my aid? When Eric left, when I had to *ask him to leave* and in the end he actually did, and I found myself alone with my daughter, and I couldn't manage all alone with my little girl, and I was *going under*, who came to my aid, who tried to save me? No one.

That's what I repeated over and over to myself: no one, no one, no one. And also: all alone, all alone.

If, I thought, I said that to the police inspector, she would, of course, be deeply offended: How can you compare the two situations, she would say. It's scandalous. They were in peril of death – and did actually die. (Or perhaps, more indulgently, believing – wrongly, of course – that she was finally reaching the nub of her psychological investigation, she would say to me: So that was it. So that was it – the trauma that explains everything and which, in fact, makes everything still more absurd. Now we've got to the root cause, she would think, satisfied at last, and at the same time, appalled.)

Of course I'd refuse to respond to her theatrical grandiloquence, and once again I would force her to reverse back out of my private life and instead I would go on watching the sea in front of me, sitting there on the rocks, while a clinging sea mist started to drop onto the beach and I shivered. Or I'd continue watching the approach from the far end of the beach of what I had at first taken to be a single jogger, but which now turned out to be two joggers, the two shapes each clearly separate, despite the drizzle starting to blur the beach, and then not after all two joggers but walkers, advancing serenely, despite the weather.

But since, once again, she would be trying to make me responsible for their deaths, whether through incompetence or ill-intent, whether by doing something wrong, or through an act of wrong-doing, and since she would fling in my face, no doubt, that the English, all this time, had rescued – I don't know how many – ninety-eight apparently, while I was letting twenty-seven drown, and this kind of point-scoring was, I suppose, intended to crush me, I would refuse to hang my head, I would not look away out of the window, as I expect she would have liked, to show her I acknowledged my defeat. No, I would not look out of the window, biting my lip.

I would then say: I hadn't saved those ones, obviously, that's true. But how many others? Why don't you listen to weeks, or years of recordings? That would be fairer. In calm weather there are on average forty boats out there trying to make the crossing. And thousands every year arrive safely in England. So how many have I saved? Let's add them up.

But it's not something you can add up. Apparently, saving is the norm, what you do, routine. It's not an extraordinary action; it's quite ordinary, not the exception but the rule. And it leaves no trace, almost as little as of the people who vanish in silence into the abyss and are absorbed, digested, sometimes even spat back out by the sea. All that is normal – as though normal life was just like that – everyone saving everyone all the time. That's how the human race survives; no need for Jesus Christ to save the world; we've been doing it perfectly well ourselves since the dawn of time, in every tiny provincial village. Salvation, if we're going to use big words, is something we offer each other every day. What a nice thought! After all, it might even be true.

Is this how the world holds together? I would have asked the police inspector, in all sincerity, if she had been something other than a police inspector – by this permanent, invisible miracle? Everyone saving everyone all the time. So that my father needn't repeat endlessly, with that naïve, admiring look he wears: My daughter saves lives, as though it was some great mystery, since everyone is saving everyone, in every moment.

But there are still some left over, Papa; there's still, always, at least one, I said. Two survived, though, I thought. Next time, let it be twenty, or even twenty-seven out of twenty-nine, not the other way round.

But it's enough for one to be lost and there is always one, there *has* to be one – and it's as if you had saved no one.

So with all this going on, this ongoing shipwreck, why bother? I asked. And why save this person rather than that one, when they are all condemned. And what justice is there? Why save one, ten, twenty; it's all the same, since you can't save them all. There is always one left. Even if you saved all of them, there would always be one left, one you didn't even know existed. And the one that you save will perish tomorrow or the day after, here or elsewhere. So why bother?

Was I actually thinking something different that night? Was it not actually that, not lethargy, as I'd said, or thought, to try to explain something in my attitude that night that deep down was incomprehensible? I couldn't exactly say how long I had had this thought, this conviction that didn't even really have the force of a conviction. But I knew it wasn't Julien who had put it in my head, or anyone else, either. He hadn't taught me what I know, that one person has to drown in order for another one to breathe properly, and that the air we breathe in is another's dying breath. That one has to be driven out so another can move in, and any place we occupy is stolen from someone we have thrown into the sea.

(People accuse me of not *putting myself in their place*, I thought once more. But the truth is exactly the opposite: I *am* in their place because I've taken their place, and the ones that drown are taking my place, and they are drowning so I can stay on the surface and I can stay on dry land while they are in the water)

Yes, why bother, I wondered, turning back towards the beach where the two walkers were making their way towards me, and they weren't walkers, I recognised them now, even at this distance; they were the two survivors of the sinking, it was clear now, so I was able to say to them, to shout out: Why bother? Because I was sure that in spite of the distance between us, and the gusts of wind sweeping the beach, they could hear me clearly and I didn't even need to shout in their direction for them to hear me. I could calmly say once again that it was just a matter of time. Soon they too would be embarked once again, on Leviathan's back, heading for extinction. There are always one or two who live to die another day, and that's why they stay on the shore, instead of finding safe refuge somewhere inland.

I saw them coming towards me, at a steady walking pace, in the gently falling rain. I didn't need to wonder what they were doing there. They thought they were coming to ask me for justice, the pair of them, to demand reparation. But what justice? Where is justice? Is there justice in the fact that someone lives instead of dying, that one person survives rather than doesn't, or rather than someone else? But I don't think it was that kind of justice they had in mind, or rather that kind of absence of justice. And they probably intended to scare me too, rising up there at the far end of the beach, steadily walking towards me. But they didn't scare me at all; there was something of the snapshot about them as though they were simply the product of my imagination, or my guilty conscience, or an allegory of my guilty conscience, and if they wanted to talk about it I didn't mind. I was happy to talk to them, just as I was happy to talk to the police inspector. I wouldn't have said anything different to what I'd said – what I would have said – to the police inspector. It wouldn't bother me, but I simply didn't want to talk to them. And so I shouted to them: I don't want to talk to you. I have nothing to say to you, I've said it all already. I've told the truth, the truth, I repeated, shouting in their direction. And then I turned back to the sea again, intending to stay there for a few more minutes, before retracing my steps homewards to make Léa's breakfast, forgetting the rest of my run for once. I wasn't going to start running in their direction.

But all the same, I thought, continuing to watch them out of the corner of my eye, why just the two of them, if they want to demand justice? Why not all the others while they're about it, the ones that died and would have even more reason to come and demand justice of me? In particular, why not the one who called me fourteen times? Where's he gone?

But maybe he isn't as dead as all that, I thought. Maybe he's floating, wandering the surface of the sea. Maybe in the end the drowned man got somewhere, after all. That's what Léa said to me, too, not that long ago, when I was talking to her again about the whole thing without realising, or maybe I didn't actually talk to her about it that time – she could just see I was thinking about it while we had breakfast, that I could see the dinghy sinking in my bowl of milky coffee, so I didn't want to drink it, like the morning before, and the morning before that, but it certainly wasn't me that raised the matter.

Whenever Eric comes to pick her up or I drop her at his place, he accuses me of talking to her about this business. Do you realise what you're doing to her, he says to me. Do you realise how much you're putting on her at her age, going on about it in front of her all the time? You'll drive her crazy, you'll destroy her. It's not healthy, it's irresponsible, etc. He says he's going to end up having to protect her from me. I must stop or he's going to have to act in Léa's interest. He says you don't tell a child of six things like that and it's wrong to drag her into my morbid fantasies, as he says I am doing. According to him, our daughter is unhappy or anxious; she thinks about the little girl that drowned because I've told her about her, and I shouldn't have. She has nightmares about it, she's worried about her mother and it's not normal for a little girl to worry about her mother. Even my own parents, according to him, are worried, etc.

But Eric was the first person who called me when the whole thing blew up, delighted of course, supposedly, to offer comfort, but really to tell me, yet again, that I should tell these high-minded lefties turning on me where to get off. I had no reason to feel guilty, and he was prepared to say good riddance to them. Listening to him, I realised that what he was really trying to find out was if I had actually done it on purpose, falling in line with his arguments, which are basically that we should just let them die, or whether I had simply arrived at a state of fatigue-induced lucidity, just saying out loud what everyone secretly thought: that after all no one asked them to leave and they should sort out their own problems, and if they thought they could turn up here and help themselves, they should at least understand that it was at their own risk and they were responsible for what happened to them. But now, it seemed, we needed to stop talking about it, and stop making such a song and dance about it, and leave our kid out of it, because she was far too young and it was unhealthy to keep going over it.

(At other times he was less vehement and even more caring, more concerned for me, as if he was finally worried on my behalf. At first he'd repeated that I had nothing to feel guilty for, and – these were his exact words – I needed to leave all that *behind me*. And then, getting concerned about my morale – though not about my morality – which, he said, didn't seem that good – he finally suggested that I should *see someone*, though it wasn't clear to me if by that he meant some kind of doctor, or even a shrink, or even a police inspector, for example. He ended by saying that I needed to give up this career, ask for a transfer, resign maybe, reminding me that on several occasions recently, and even before *these sad events*, I had expressed a wish to leave my job. All I could say to this was that, in any case, this was being done for me, given the way things were going, with the opening not just of a judicial enquiry but of an internal procedure too, aimed at determining, as they put it, whether a negligence had occurred.)

But that morning I had actually said nothing to Léa, and I almost never do now. I've stopped talking to her about it, I've stopped talking about it to anyone. I'll only talk about it with the police inspector, if I'm summoned, as it seems I will be, or if I go of my own accord before that. But I don't speak to my little one about it any more. And she was the one who wanted to talk about it, not me, she who put her hand on mine, next to my coffee bowl, and said to me with a stricken look, as if I was the little girl and I had lost my teddy: Maybe he wasn't dead, he hadn't drowned, the boy who called me fourteen times that night and who ended his fourteenth call with the words: It's finished.

(And that time I did remember the word, which of course you hear on the recordings, that last word, unconsciously theatrical: It's finished, but I couldn't determine his tone of voice and consequently his exact intention, but above all it struck me as paradoxical, because though it probably was finished for him, it was just starting for me, unless in one sense it was also finished for me too.)

So maybe he hadn't perished, but instead had begun to swim when all the others were probably dead already or almost, and were vanishing beneath the waves. And while they all lay scattered round the debris of the boat, he began swimming, swimming tirelessly, immortal, saved for ever and swimming hour after hour without ceasing, without wearying, till the small hours of the morning, crossing the Channel, braving the deadly wake of the tankers, the troughs and swirls they stir up, ignoring the icy cold, swimming on and on and crossing the sea and finally reaching the shore, shipwrecked but safe and sound. Imagine maybe that he hadn't landed on the English coast, she said, but on a kind of island, far far away, after wandering on the surface of the sea and crossing other seas beside the Channel. That he was finally thrown up on a distant, foreign shore, and maybe in the end, she went on, welcomed by the inhabitants of the island. They would think he was the king they had lost, whose disappearance had left them anxious and helpless. They'd think he looked like this vanished king, astonishingly like; they'd be happy they'd got their king back and he would agree to pretend to be him, so that the shipwrecked man now became a king, through a misunderstanding, though far from his own country and with no hope of ever returning there, but anyway king now of a faraway country. The migrant become king, an innocent impostor who had only ever dreamed of working in a corner shop in London, now agreeing to govern this people, to rule justly and well, loved by his people, and having found happiness.

But in reality, he sank gently to the bottom, dragged down by his waterlogged shoes, weighed down by his clothes, suffocating, his lungs full of water, his panic-stricken heart finally stopped dead by the cold. Down, down, he went to the sandy bed of the sea. And gently he placed one foot on the sand, then the other, inert, weightless, like an astronaut on the Moon, at the bottom of the sea. For a while he stayed still, looking about him, then began to walk, to move forward through the tall seaweed and sleepy fish. And as he walks, others join him, also sinking to the sea bed, one by one, their feet landing on the sand, one by one, all twenty-seven of them, landing gently at the sea bottom, walking behind him now as in a dream, silent and slow, with him up ahead, advancing, light of foot, them following, accompanying him, and presumably others, all the others, join them too, gradually over time, all those who have been swallowed up, the already wrecked whose wrecking is completed by the sea. There would be dozens of them, dozens upon dozens, perhaps from every sea on earth, an entire population of drowned people. All of them setting forth beneath hundreds of fathoms of water, heedless now of the outlines, far above them on the surface, of the supertankers and cargo ships which pass, scarcely visible, like the shadows of huge fish. And in the thin green-blue light of the deep, they find their way.

Yes, I thought, standing at the water's edge, with the waves reaching the tips of my trainers, straining unsuccessfully to casually seize me, to wrap around my ankles, to make me fall by taking away the sand beneath my feet and dragging me off, yes I could hand myself in at the Cherbourg Coastguard office, without waiting for a summons, and I'd ask to speak to the police inspector in charge of the enquiry instead of just talking to myself as I do every day, looking at the sea as if the twenty-seven people were finally going to emerge from it after their underwater odyssey and stand there before me. I would hear my voice recorded instead of in my head and I would have someone other than myself sitting opposite, and if I chanced to look through the window I would see something other than the sea – the dry land we stand on, not the shifting element that absorbs everything and on which nothing can be built, which cancels out everything, forever. I would see, for example, a construction site, not ruins and bits of wreckage.

I could do that. I could have.

But in the end I dismissed the idea because in any case it was as if I had already handed myself in at the police station, as if I had already spoken to the inspector, had said everything I had to say, and this interview had led to nothing, had had no consequences, so I won't hand myself over to the Cherbourg police. I won't start a conversation with the two people still coming towards me through the mist, who are in no hurry, it seems, and perhaps don't actually want to talk to me. Perhaps they are coming not to demand justice (what justice, I repeated) but rather to administer justice, do justice, or even to take the law into their own hands, as the saying goes, which is the precise opposite of justice, but anyway, and given the circumstances, shouldn't I just throw myself into the sea and drown? The B movie aspect to this hypothesis, feasible though it seemed, made me smile. But in any case, I said, watching the water swirl up around my feet, I'll have left before they get to this point.

Am I really all alone on this shore? I wasn't saying that just because I saw the two of them coming towards me, and was therefore not alone on the beach. Nor did I say it because I was thinking of the CROSS surveillance post, that sort of overlooks the shore, where I'm really not alone, although everyone apparently wants me to be, so I can carry the can. In fact, I didn't actually say it at all. I said it *generally speaking*, and now the foul sea mist was changing into a fine drizzle, gradually drenching my face.

Who is here on the shore? Who is watching this shipwreck from the mainland? Is it really just me, no one else? That would suit everyone, but don't you believe it: I am not here alone on the shore; I'm not alone watching this unending 'drama at sea' from a safe distance, night after night. And I'm not just referring to Julien, behind me, complacently thinking about Pascal and the misery of mankind, who no longer believes in God because God mass-produces migrants, then drowns them in the sea like kittens, so he can fall into noble despair. While I'm standing here on dry land, there are all the others at my back, so many of them, thousands, millions of people.

The entire world is there, the entire actual world at my back, on the shore.

Even my father is there, sitting at the lunch table, there on the beach, with his kindly smile. You are all there. If I turned round I would see you all, sunk into your sofas on the sand, in your deck chairs, in your offices, watching without watching, while I keep my vigil like an idiot, and afterwards, once the drama is over, lashing out, saying: It's a scandal, It's revolting. And yet that night I saw not one of them jump into the water to help, not one offering to reinflate the rubber dinghy with his own feeble lungs. But when it comes to protesting and calling other people monsters, then everyone has enough breath.

There is no shipwreck without spectators. Even when there's no one, when it's far out at sea, at night, without witnesses, even when there's no living soul in sight for thousands of nautical miles, only waves and the viscous night, covering everything, swallowing everything; when there are no more eyes to see than there are arms to reach out, there are still spectators and the shore from which they are watching is never far away, even if, at the same time, it is infinitely distant. Even with their eyes shut, people are still watching, and I can't think of a single one who could say: I wasn't there. From inside their own homes, they are all watching the drama, and the drama is never-ending; it plays out every day, every night, on high days and holidays, even when they're doing other things, they're still spectators of the 'drama at sea'.

Blind spectators and a spectacle for the blind. They watch, they see nothing; in fact they can't see anything. The stage is blacked out, and at this distance, from their sofas or in front of their TVs, they can't make anything out. They see nothing, but are still present at the drama. I am the only one with opera glasses, who sees. But not one person in the audience asks me to lend them my glasses, not one wants to step onto the darkened stage, not one looks like getting up to step into the water.

There's only me who sees and hears and who responds. And to the blind man, spitting on me as he finishes his copious lunch with colleagues and goes back to his little office, I'll say: Hey, jerk, see that guy sleeping in a cardboard box at the foot of your building? He's rowing across the tarmac, he's sinking too. But he's not dozens of kilometres out at sea, at dead of night, he is quite easy to geolocate, he's just in front of your feet. So are you going to send him help or is that my job again?

Who sleeps in that dead of night, and who keeps awake as the disaster unfolds? Who hears? Who stands at my side while I keep watch and listen out? No one's here helping me. No one's saving me. I hold my daughter tight in my arms at night, my head on her shoulder, but her regular breathing does not mask the sound that comes up from the sea. The night is full of voices calling, mingling with the sound of the waves which do not cradle me. All these voices like waves above the waves. Voices of men, women, cries, sobs, prayers and farewells. A great babbling in English, always the same words, the beseeching sea.

I cling to my daughter's body like a lifebuoy, but it doesn't save me.

I know people would have liked me to say: You're not going to die, I'll save you. And not because I would have actually saved them, done my job, done the necessary, sent rescue. Not because I'd done what you're meant to do. They wanted me to have *said* it, at least to have said it, just to have said the words. That was what the investigator was waiting for anxiously, for everyone to *hear*, to hear their own voice in mine in these recordings. The voice of each of us saying I will save you. Each one in my place. The voice of the whole of humanity reassured to hear itself saying, uttering the words: I will save you; you will not die – not actually saving, no one cares about that, not acting, not even helping. But at least saying it, because to fail to say those words is to be less than human. In the end, whether they drowned or not didn't matter; what mattered were my words. What mattered was not that they were saved; it was that I should be saved, and the whole world with me, through these words. Saved by my own words, not condemned by them.

But I said: You will not be saved.

And if, listening to the recording, the investigator turns her gaze away, unable look at me, with that sad, devastated look in her eyes, it's because it's not me she'll hear, but herself and everyone along with her, saying: I will not save you, while she wanted to hear me say the opposite – wanted it *for herself,* for everyone, so humanity could be reassured about itself, so humanity need not doubt its humanity, and so she would not have to fear what she'd become, that is to say, a woman like me, like the one I've become.

But I didn't say it, I didn't say: You will not die, I will save you. Basically I said the opposite.

Well yes, it's true I thought, as I entered the cold water, it's true. I said that phrase when the communication went down, or perhaps even before it went down. It was crackling. He was saying What? What? He asked me for the umpteenth time to say it again. So yes, I did utter that phrase, the recordings confirm it. It was perhaps a way of saying Farewell, or Cheers. Cheers is perhaps not the right term, now I think of it. Not a very friendly, Cheers, it's true, but he didn't hear me, at his end. The line had gone dead. Listening to it with me, the investigator had turned her eyes away, and there must have been a heavy silence, she must have looked distressed.

I don't know if I regret saying those words, I thought, with the water already up to my waist. But what's stupid is I now don't know if it was me that said them or him at the other end, still talking to me though the water was up to his waist. Now I think about it, it's as if I was hearing the words, instead of saying them, as if they were addressed to me. They echo in my ears, in my head, from beyond, from the sea and the night, from the even darker night within me, from the depths. I don't really understand the meaning of them, and that bothers me. I mean I don't know which way they are going: from him to me or from me to him.

I can say it back to you, if you like, the phrase you hear in the recordings, that I hear in my head. That is exactly what I said, but perhaps it was him saying it as he drowned, with his mouth full of seawater, holding his silent phone above his head as he went down, just as we lost contact. I could hear nothing, wanted to hear nothing, because I had heard without hearing. I said or he said to me: You're not hearing me, you will not be saved.

About the Author, Translator and Introducer

Vincent Delecroix (born 1969 in Paris) is a French philosopher and writer. A graduate of the École normale supérieure, and *agrégé* in philosophy, he teaches at the École Pratique des Hautes Études. Vincent Delecroix received the Prix Valery Larbaud in 2007 for his novel *Ce qui est perdu* (published in 2006) and the Grand prix de littérature de l'Académie française after he published *Tombeau d'Achille* (in 2008). *Small Boat* (*Naufrage*) was on the longlist of the 2023 Prix Goncourt. This is the first translation of a novel by Vincent Delecroix in English.

Helen Stevenson studied Modern languages (German and French) at Oxford University, and has been translating literary texts from French to English for twenty-five years; translations include *Black Moses* by Alain Mabanckou (shortlisted for the Man Booker International Prize 2017), *The Missing Piece* by Antoine Bello and *My Phantom Husband* by Marie Darrieussecq. She is also a writer of novels including *Mad Elaine* and *Love Like Salt; A Memoir*. She spent much of her adult life prior to Brexit in France, in Céret (Pyrénées Orientales) and Cajarc (Lot). She now lives in Somerset in South West England.

Jeremy Harding is a contributing editor at the *London Review of Books*, where he has written often about the Maghreb and the Middle East. His books include *Border Vigils: Keeping Migrants out of the Rich World*, and *Mother Country*. A collection of essays *Analogue Africa: Notes on the Anti-Colonial Imagination* is forthcoming in 2026.

ABOUT

MARINER BOOKS

MARINER BOOKS traces its beginnings to 1832 when William Ticknor cofounded the Old Corner Bookstore in Boston, from which he would run the legendary firm Ticknor and Fields, publisher of Ralph Waldo Emerson, Harriet Beecher Stowe, Nathaniel Hawthorne, and Henry David Thoreau. Following Ticknor's death, Henry Oscar Houghton acquired Ticknor and Fields and, in 1880, formed Houghton Mifflin, which later merged with venerable Harcourt Publishing to form Houghton Mifflin Harcourt. HarperCollins purchased HMH's trade publishing business in 2021 and reestablished their storied lists and editorial team under the name Mariner Books.

Uniting the legacies of Houghton Mifflin, Harcourt Brace, and Ticknor and Fields, Mariner Books continues one of the great traditions in American bookselling. Our imprints have introduced an incomparable roster of enduring classics, including Hawthorne's *The Scarlet Letter,* Thoreau's *Walden,* Willa Cather's *O Pioneers!,* Virginia Woolf's *To the Lighthouse,* W.E.B. Du Bois's *Black Reconstruction,* J.R.R. Tolkien's *The Lord of the Rings,* Carson McCullers's *The Heart Is a Lonely Hunter,* Ann Petry's *The Narrows,* George Orwell's *Animal Farm* and *Nineteen Eighty-Four,* Rachel Carson's *Silent Spring,* Margaret Walker's *Jubilee,* Italo Calvino's *Invisible Cities,* Alice Walker's *The Color Purple,* Margaret Atwood's *The Handmaid's Tale,* Tim O'Brien's *The Things They Carried,* Philip Roth's *The Plot Against America,* Jhumpa Lahiri's *Interpreter of Maladies,* and many others. Today Mariner Books remains proudly committed to the craft of fine publishing established nearly two centuries ago at the Old Corner Bookstore.